# THE HOUSE ON STONE'S THROW ISLAND

# THE HOUSE ON STONE'S THROW ISLAND

## DAN POBLOCKI

SCHOLASTIC PRESS · NEW YORK

Library of Congress Cataloging-in-Publication Data available

ISBN 978-0-545-64556-0

10 9 8 7 6 5 4 3 2 1          15 16 17 18 19

Printed in the U.S.A.   23
First edition, September 2015

Book design by Christopher Stengel

*For Daniel,*

*who helps me weather the storms*

# OCEAN OF GLASS

# CHAPTER ONE

THE FERRY DEPARTED from Haggspoint Harbor into the still waters of the bay early Friday morning, two days before the wedding. A group of nine travelers huddled at the bow of the boat, wrapped in layers of cardigans and shawls and cotton scarves, clutching the iron railing as a salty breeze tousled their hair. Their luggage was piled on several wide wooden benches behind them. They sipped steaming cups of coffee, tea, and hot chocolate, though the fresh air was more bracing than the caffeine.

Despite the chill in the September air and the ocean spray that dampened their skin, it was a beautiful morning. The forecast had called for sunny skies — a perfect weekend for a wedding — so no one on the boat had any notion of the storm that would rise up later that evening. The ferry glided smoothly past the jagged rocks of the coastline. Tall pine trees stretched up from the land, packed tightly together. A bald eagle screeched. Several in the group oohed and aahed in surprise, pointing toward the bird's nest perched atop a tall barren trunk, unaware that by the next morning, the nest would be gone, taken out by the torrential rains and the gusts of wind that would also impede electricity, communication, and travel between the mainland and the many islands off the coast.

Behind the wheel, up on the bridge, the ferry captain stared into the peach haze of sunrise, setting a southeasterly course, steering as best as he could around the hundreds of lobster buoys that speckled the surface of the bay like colorful pieces of candy. The captain was a grizzled-looking but jovial man. His one crew member, his eighteen-year-old grandson, was hiding in the cabin below, reading a comic book, waiting to dock at the next wharf. The *Sea Witch* wasn't nearly as large as the ferries that delivered mail and sundries to the islands closest to the coast, but it was a good size for a private party like this one. Those other ships never journeyed out to the farther islands, especially islands with a single, extravagant home like the one on Stone's Throw Island, where he was now headed, completely unaware that the *Sea Witch* would be gone tomorrow, wrecked on a shoal off Haggspoint. If he'd suspected that a third of his current passengers would never set foot on the mainland again, he'd have turned the boat around immediately.

The wedding planner, a bubbly and bubble-shaped woman named Margo Lintel, had arranged this ride, as well as several more throughout the weekend. Margo stepped away from the small crowd and sat perched on the edge of a bench, disguising her clenched anxiety behind her businesslike face. She scanned her notebook, checking off completed tasks and writing down new ones. So far everything was going perfectly, but there was still a lot to do. She would not function half as well if not for her assistant — a young, bearded, and bespectacled man with narrow shoulders and a prominent gut — Gregory Elliott.

"The caterers confirmed the live lobster delivery for Sunday morning," Gregory whispered in Margo's ear while glancing at his cell phone. "Gagnon said he'd help me arrange the fire pit, and the seaweed planks tomorrow night. Everything according to plan. And the forecast is still clear."

"Good. Great." Margo nodded, jotting his words in her notebook. "Thank you, Gregory. Make sure everyone is comfortable, yes?"

Gregory smiled and headed back toward the group.

Margo flipped through a few pages searching for the guest list, glancing up at the company at the bow, trying to place names with faces. There was nothing more embarrassing than calling the groom's mother by the name of the bride. Soon, she found what she was looking for:

The Sandovals
    Bruno, the groom
    Vivian, his mother
    Josie, his little sister
    Carlos, his father (arriving Saturday with the grandmother)

The Barkers
    Aimee, the bride
    Otis, her father
    Cynthia, her mother
    Elias (Eli), her little brother

The youngest two stood on opposite sides of the group, both staring into the distance. Josie and Eli. According to her notes, they were both starting seventh grade next week, in different schools, in different cities. They'd only just met on the wharf back at Haggspoint, and here they were already pretending that the other did not exist. Margo made a mental note to nudge the kids together once they reached the island. It was her job to make sure everyone had fun this weekend, not just the bride and groom.

She had no clue how quickly the coming storm would drag this idea away in a whirlpool of terror, spiraling it down into the depths of her memory, soon to be forgotten entirely.

# CHAPTER TWO

FORTY MINUTES LATER, much of the morning mist had burned away. The ferry had passed the last of the lobster-trap buoys a mile back. The water reflected the sky's hazy blue so seamlessly that the horizon was nearly invisible until a dark patch emerged in the distance.

The island.

"Ooh, look!" said Aimee, the bride.

"Is that it?" asked Bruno, the groom.

Their families, who had earlier dispersed to the benches to chat and rest, rushed back to the bow's railing.

"That is the place," said Margo, following them. "Lovely, no?"

"It's perfect," said Aimee. "Oh, this is so wonderful!" To Margo's surprise, the young woman turned and hugged her so tightly Margo almost yelped.

"Looks the same as any other island up here," said Eli quietly, as if to himself. Josie, the groom's little sister, glanced at him quizzically, then released a small chuckle. He squinted at her, as if worried that she were secretly judging him, or maybe making fun. But she had already turned her back, not giving him a chance to figure her out. His face turned red.

"But it's not like any other island," said Gregory, Margo's assistant. "The house's size alone makes it unique. Look. You can just see it now."

As the ferry got closer, Margo felt her heart flutter. Wooden pilings rose out of low-tide water, making the wharf appear taller than it had in Gregory's photographs. Along the shore, sharp boulders created a wall-like periphery. There was no beach out here, only a fifteen-foot drop from the land to rocks that collected greenish tidal pools below. From the wharf, a gravel path stretched up a long grassy expanse toward the stone building at the top of the steep incline. The house was more beautiful than she'd hoped. It looked like something out of a Jane Austen novel — that or one of the famous "cottages" in Newport, Rhode Island, the majestic summer homes that weren't cottages at all but modern castles built by the richest families of the northeastern United States during the late nineteenth and early twentieth centuries.

Margo had read that the current owner had outfitted the building with modern amenities. An oil drum provided heat and hot water. An underwater cable ran to the mainland for electricity. She imagined that the party would be perfectly comfortable, if not indulged.

Gregory's original description of the house as a two-story rectangular box was accurate, but it also seemed epically unfair to the grandeur of its Greek Revival embellishments. Or, Margo wondered, was the style Italianate? She'd encountered a few similar examples up and down the coast of Maine — beautiful, white, dressed with curlicues of stone, like the frosting on a wedding cake. Enormous lead-paned windows, half-moons at their tops, ran symmetrically along the first floor. Six to the left side of the front door. Six to the right. Smaller square windows decorated the top floor. Below, Ionic columns supported a heavy stone overhang at the main entrance. From there, wide stone steps led down to a marble trail that wrapped around a fountain where an oxidized copper fox and hawk were frozen in a desperate clash for survival.

At the bottom of the hill, a smaller, two-story structure stood beside the wharf — a boathouse or an extremely large shed — covered in weathered gray clapboard and trimmed with white. It was more traditionally New England than the mansion up the hill.

This must have been where the extra guest accommodations that Margo had arranged were located.

*Lovely view*, thought Margo, wishing that she could take one of the rooms out there for herself. *All this water!*

The caretakers' team had done a magnificent job of keeping the grounds in shape. The grass was trim. The gardens bloomed with late-summer flowers — an explosion of orange and pink and purple. Margo made out several men clustered together on the immense lawn, dressed in dark uniforms, standing still, watching as the boat approached the wharf. She waved at them, certain that they could see her, but none of them waved back. They only continued to stare, unmoving. For a moment, she wondered if the figures were actually statues. Margo felt a chill breach her insulated jacket and tickle her skin.

The captain blew the horn, a resounding call that echoed off the water in all directions. The party floundered momentarily, falling away from one another in surprise, as if a bomb had gone off. But Margo raised a hand and spoke up, and they paid attention, glad to have a leader. "Gather your belongings! We disembark shortly!"

A few minutes later, the captain's grandson and first mate, Rick, had secured two sturdy ropes to the dock's moorings and pulled the boat snugly against the platform. He pushed the metal footbridge away from the boat deck and opened the inner gate. The excited party shuttled off the ferry and climbed up onto the wharf.

Before they followed the crowd, Margo and Gregory met with the captain to double-check contact information. "You'll not get any cell service out here," said the captain, whose name was Sonny Thayer, "and you probably already know that the house has a two-way radio for emergencies. I don't expect you'll need to use it before I return tomorrow morning with the other guests."

"No, I don't expect we will," said Margo.

"Enjoy the day. Supposed to be beautiful. Wish I could stay."

"We do too," said Gregory. "Thanks for everything, Sonny."

Margo kissed Rick's cheek and then bounded across the footbridge.

# CHAPTER THREE

THE PARTY HAD GATHERED where the dock met the island's gravel path. A white golf cart was parked there, and a diminutive man was loading luggage onto a platform at the rear of the vehicle. "Might have to make a couple trips," Margo heard the man say. His voice was high-pitched, as if trapped in his bulbous nose. "Unless you folks don't mind walking," he added.

A small metal dinghy bobbed in the water near the rocks. Its little outboard motor was tilted up out of the surf. Margo figured it belonged to the caretakers, in case they needed to leave the island, though she couldn't imagine making the crossing in a boat that looked like an oversize bathtub.

"Walking is good for the lungs," said Vivian Sandoval, the groom's mother. "And the air out here is magnificent. C'mon, Josie. It's not far." Her daughter smiled reluctantly and lifted a duffel bag from the ground.

"Eli will join you," said Otis Barker, the bride's father. "Won't you, Eli?"

"But I wanted to ride on the cart with Aimee," said Eli, sounding hurt.

His mother, Cynthia, rubbed his shoulder. "Give Aimee some space. Go on. Get to know your new sister, okay?"

"Technically, she's not my —"

The bride sidled up next to him and stared him down. "Grow *up*, Eli," Aimee answered through her teeth, her voice a sing-songy threat.

Eli blinked, shooting a glance at Josie and her mother, and then retrieved his suitcase from the back of the golf cart.

"Mr. Gagnon!" Margo called out with extra cheer. The little man stood on the footrail of the golf cart to see who was bellowing his name, then hopped off and pushed through the group, sticking out his hand at her.

"You must be the wedding planner. Mrs. Lintel?"

"Margo."

"Call me Charlie." He turned to the rest of the party and introduced himself as one of the caretakers. "My wife and I are so happy that you chose Stone's Throw Island."

Aimee and Bruno clasped each other's waists and grinned. "So are we," they answered. Otis raised a small camera and snapped their picture. The top of Aimee's head, a wild mop of red curls, just barely met the height of Bruno's broad shoulders. His own dark features stood in stark contrast to her paleness. They were an attractive couple.

Margo leaned close to Charlie. "I was hoping we may have some time this morning to go over a few things."

"Of course. Of course. Time is all we have out here."

"Splendid. Your men have done a wonderful job on the property. It looks like something out of a fairy tale. The blossoms. The lawn. The fountain! My goodness!"

"My men?"

"Your crew," Margo said, glancing up the hill where she'd seen the men standing, watching as the boat had approached. They were gone now. "They must have been working around the clock. I saw three or four of them from the ferry. Will they be staying in the house as well?" Charlie Gagnon turned and looked into her eyes. When Margo'd first seen him, she would have guessed he was in his midsixties. Now, confusion weighed down the papery skin of his face, giving him the appearance of a man ten years older. "What is it?" she asked. "What's wrong?"

He shook his head. "Beatrice and I have no crew. *We're* the caretakers. No one else has been on the island today until you all showed up just now."

"But the men . . ." Margo gazed up the hill again. The space the men had occupied contained a shadowy residue, which she blinked away. She was certain she'd seen figures watching her.

Now, it seemed as though only the house on the hill was looking back. Those windows with the half-moon tops were like several pairs of surprised eyes.

"No men," Charlie said, shaking his head sharply. "No crew. Only me and my wife."

Margo felt something gurgle in her stomach. From somewhere in the distance, there came a low rumble. Was that thunder? She pulled her gaze away from the house and glanced out at the horizon. The ocean was a crystal mirror reflecting the endless blue sky. Not a cloud in sight.

Sonny's ferry had already motored several hundred feet away from the wharf, turned now toward Haggspoint. Margo fought the sudden urge to run to the end of the dock and shout for him to come back. Instead, she shook out her arms and legs, and took a deep breath.

"Well then," she said to Charlie, keeping her face as placid as the gulf water, "I am impressed."

# RIPPLES

# CHAPTER FOUR

ELI'S STOMACH HAD felt fine during the boat trip, but now that he was back on land, he was struck with an annoying queasiness. He wasn't sure if the strange sensation had been caused by the ride or by his sister's outburst. *Grow up, Eli!* she'd said to him — in front of everyone!

Dragging his suitcase up the hill, Eli realized that the nauseated feeling was transforming. His cheeks flushed. His heart pounded. In his mind, he couldn't stop replaying memories of when he and Aimee had been younger, playing hours of Bomberman on their old Xbox, before she became obsessed with boys and motorcycles and her sorority and finally Bruno, after which it was apparent Eli wasn't worth her time anymore. Except to scream at.

And now everyone expected him to simply welcome a new "sister" with open arms? Josie Sandoval: the girl who smirked whenever he said anything. Yeah, right.

On the path to the house, as Eli walked in silence, a golf cart zoomed past, its tires tossing a small spray of stones in its wake. He leaped out of its way, onto the dewy grass. Eli was about to shout a piece of his mind, when he realized that his companions, Vivian and Josie, were staring at him. "That was close," said Vivian, her soft voice an antidote to the poison of his sudden frustration.

"Too close," Eli mumbled. "Geez. What an —" Charlie Gagnon, the caretaker, who was behind the cart's wheel, called an apology over his shoulder. It had all happened so quickly, Eli barely had time to register his embarrassment. "Sorry," he said. "Everyone all right?"

"Totally fine," said Josie, that smirk decorating her face again, this time seeming to pass a hidden message. *You almost swore in front of my mom!*

Eli had to keep himself from smiling back. He didn't want her to think they were friends now.

Several hundred feet back down the hill, Eli's parents waited on the wharf with Margo's assistant for Charlie to return and pick them up. If Otis had heard what Eli had almost just said, he'd have sent Eli to his quarters for the rest of the day before forcing him to make a public apology at dinner that evening.

Vivian Sandoval blinked, reading the worry in Eli's forehead, and then waved the group forward to follow her up the path. "We'll just have to watch out for the cart on its way back down. Apparently, a driving test isn't required to operate one of those things." Eli laughed, grasping the handle of his suitcase harder so that it wouldn't slip out of his sweaty palm. "So, Eli?" Vivian went on, dragging her own luggage, flipping her silver-colored shoulder-length hair away from her face. "You were about to tell us all about yourself?"

"I was?"

"Well, if you weren't, I think now's a good time to start, you know, before you're run down by another golf cart in the prime of your youth."

Eli smiled, then glanced ahead at Josie, who seemed determined to keep her vision focused on the ground. Her long brown hair hung limply past her wide, bony shoulders. She was obviously embarrassed by her mother's boldness.

"There's not much to tell," said Eli. Of course there was, but where was he supposed to start? *I'm turning thirteen in December. My favorite subject in school is English. I'm writing a graphic novel with my best friend about an invisible dolphin with telekinetic powers. I accidentally killed my pet hamster in the spring by leaving its cage too close to an open window one night.* "I'm happy to be here."

"Mm. What a polite thing to say. Josie, isn't Eli *polite?*"

Eli slowed. Was she making fun of him? Adults weren't supposed to do that to kids, were they? Not so blatantly anyway.

"Very polite," said Josie, keeping her eyes fixed on the path.

Vivian turned back to look at him, raising an eyebrow as if daring him to challenge her. He wasn't one to turn down a challenge, not from someone other than his father. "Did you hear what the weird old wedding planner was telling the caretaker back at the wharf?" he asked. Vivian shook her head. "She said she saw a whole bunch of people watching us from the shore as the boat approached. And the caretaker told her that no one else was on the island but him and his wife. Bizarre, right?" There. How polite was that?

Vivian's face lit up. "Very bizarre. Did *you* see any people watching us, Eli?"

"Nope," he said, struggling to keep up with Josie, who was now several steps ahead. The group was almost halfway to the house's front door. "But it doesn't surprise me. What the wedding planner said she saw. A lot of these islands out here have some really odd histories. People tell stories."

This got Josie's attention. She glanced over her shoulder. "Really? Like what?"

"Oh, the usual. Ghosts. Weird lights. Sea monsters!" He smiled. "All sorts of fantastical phenomena."

Eli had grown up many miles inland. The most interesting of the island stories had traveled from the gulf and the bays to the people of the suburban towns as if swirling up the tidal estuaries that stabbed into Maine's immense jagged coast. Many of the folks who had houses out on the islands lived there only part-time, and they brought their legends home with them in the off-season.

"*Fantastical phenomena,*" Vivian echoed. "You're a poet, Eli."

"The creepiest story I've heard is about a family that inhabits a deserted island out here somewhere. The family usually lives off the fish they catch around the shore. But sometimes they've been known to leave their island to go hunting for . . . *different* food." Eli paused, knowing the response that would eventually come.

Josie was the one who asked, "And what kind of food would that be?"

"Humans," Eli said.

"That's disgusting," she said, suddenly speeding her pace up the hill.

Vivian chuckled. "He was joking, honey. Josie! Slow down."

Eli didn't answer. Of course he wasn't joking — by fifth grade, every kid he'd gone to school with had heard the story of the feral cannibal family — but he decided not to say anything more about it at the moment. It was one thing to be called *polite* by a couple of strangers at your sister's wedding. *Polite* implied you were slightly boring. Ordinary. Plain. *Polite* meant your parents should be proud of you. Being called *disgusting*, however, was another thing entirely. Eli smiled to himself, unsure at this point which he preferred.

# CHAPTER FIVE

THE CARETAKER'S WIFE greeted them at the house's entrance. She stood almost six feet tall and was as skinny as a scarecrow, in a floor-length pale pink dress, shapeless and sack-like. Her long gray hair was twisted tightly into a bun that sat on top of her head. There was something about her that at first made Eli nervous, but when she said, "Welcome," her smile was so honest and kind, he relaxed a bit, loosening the grip on the handle of his case. In one delicate hand, she held up a small metal tray on which she'd balanced three glass flutes filled with golden liquid. "Champagne for the mother of the groom. And sparkling apple for the kids."

Eli felt his skin flush. *Kids? Really, lady?* It made him think of Aimee's outburst. *Which is it, people? Am I a kid? Or should I grow up?* Glancing briefly at Josie to see if she was having a similar reaction (she wasn't — her expression was blank and mysterious), he placed his suitcase by the others that sat just inside the foyer. Josie and Vivian did the same, then graciously took their glasses.

"I'm Beatrice Gagnon," the woman said. "Come in, please. Everyone is starting to gather in the solarium."

"Well, thank you," said Vivian, raising her glass to Beatrice, then clinking it against Josie's and Eli's. "This is all very nice."

"Nice?" Beatrice sniffed, then glanced around the great marble foyer wearing a look that said Vivian had used a ten-cent word to describe something that she considered priceless. The room was a perfect white cube. The ceiling soared nearly thirty feet. An elaborate crystal chandelier hung just over their heads, a dozen arms reaching out from its center like some ornately festooned insect.

Dual staircases hugged the white walls on either side of the double walnut doors, meeting at a second-floor landing. Tall ferns fanned out from fat white ceramic pots that sat on each side of the balcony. A doorway beyond the wide marble banister above led to a tunnel of darkness where the bedrooms were hidden behind closed doors. "Well, yes, I suppose it is *nice*. Come along now. Don't want to keep everyone waiting."

Eli peered out the front door and watched as Charlie's cart rumbled back down the hill to pick up his parents and Margo's assistant at the wharf. "They could've walked," he whispered to himself. As the ferry had approached the shore, Eli had imagined that the island contained a type of enchantment — not literally, of course — but it seemed charming enough to captivate a couple of dyed-in-the-wool Mainers. Back on the mainland, they would have scoffed at the idea of a two-hundred-yard golf-cart shuttle ride, but here, the luxury made them wide-eyed with wonder. Maybe the island's magic would make everyone more pleasant for the weekend?

"Eli?" Josie called to him from the arched entry just below the staircase's landing. Beatrice and Vivian had already gone ahead. "You coming?" It was the first thing she'd said to him all morning that didn't make him want to pull the hood of his jacket over his head and hide — the first time her smile didn't seem like a weapon.

"Oh. Yeah." He slugged down what was left in his glass. "It's just . . . I think this stuff has gone to my head already."

"Right," said Josie, drawing out the word. "Apple juice can be *so* intoxicating."

# CHAPTER SIX

TWENTY MINUTES LATER, the entire wedding party, except for Margo, had gathered in the room off the back of the house, the one that Beatrice called the solarium. Its walls and ceiling were made up entirely of large panes of glass attached by thin strips of a dark metal. The floor was a brick patio. The room was shaded by several tall pines that stood outside across a small patch of grass. The ocean was visible through the branches, glistening in the morning light. Inside, the air was warm and humid — a welcome sensation after the damp chill of the boat ride. A strong scent of flowers was apparent, though Eli saw none.

"Obviously, the name is a joke," said Eli's father. A tall, wide man, Otis Barker stood beside his wife, resting his hands on his round stomach. "It has to be. Stone's Throw Island? We're a dozen miles from the coast at least."

"Out here, we're actually closer to Nova Scotia than to Maine," said Bruno, patting Aimee's hand. "I looked it up."

"A joke," said Charlie Gagnon, who stood in the kitchen doorway across the hall. "You could look at it that way. This land has had many names over the years. I can't remember what the natives called it once upon a time. Stone's Throw is the latest iteration, a remnant from the last owner's tenure. The new owners thought it was quaint, so they kept it."

Eli sat beside Josie on a small wicker love seat, his knees squeezed together, his hands clenched tightly in his lap. The adults — his sister and her fiancé included — had helped themselves to more champagne, and they all appeared to be getting a little giddy. Faces were flushed, and tongues were wagging. Eli was glad he was too young to participate. He wasn't sure what he'd say if he didn't have total control over himself. Maybe he'd have shared his annoyance that he hadn't been allowed to invite his best friend, Shane Mullins. Or that his phone had no service here. Or that the only other person here his age was a girl whose occasional gaze made him feel like a weirdo. He'd gotten similar glances at school from his classmates last year whenever they overheard him conspiring with Shane about the graphic novel they were making together.

Or maybe he'd say something even worse if he'd had champagne, something about his selfish sister, something about her fiancé's plastic smile.

"Who are the owners?" asked Eli's mother, Cynthia. Her voice was as thin as her frame. Wavy dyed-blond hair hung lifelessly from her head, and large diamond-drop earrings dangled from her earlobes.

"You mean, *what* are the owners?" Charlie laughed, a private joke between he and himself. "The island was bought last year by a small financial corporation down in Portland. An investment, I suppose, to rent us out for special events. We've had five weddings and two birthday parties this past summer. Even so, this island is still our home. Beatrice and I have lived here since the eighties, when we were hired by the previous owners. They rarely visited. Their loss!"

Cynthia leaned forward, a wide grin on her face. "Maybe you two will still be here in ten years . . . for Josie and Eli! Wouldn't that just be the cutest? Can we book this far in advance?"

Eli froze, eyes wide with horror.

A moment later, the group caught on, their laughter resounding off the glass walls and ceiling. Even Josie pretended to chuckle. But from the corner of his eye, Eli noticed her jaw tighten as she clenched the arm of the love seat.

"I hope you don't think me a busybody for asking about the house," Cynthia said to Beatrice, as if already forgetting her own joke. "I was just curious."

"Of course not, honey," said Beatrice, continuing to chuckle. "This is our *job*. Free rent. They pay us to maintain the place. We were worried when we learned we were being sold last year. Thankfully, the corporation kept Charlie and me on. And, after being isolated for so long, we love having guests!"

"Oh, let's not talk about rent and money and such things," said Margo, pushing past Charlie and Beatrice into the solarium, waving her hands about as if to clear away a stink. Her cheeks looked especially red, Eli thought. Maybe she'd had some of the champagne too. "How about we show everyone to their rooms?"

"Wait," said Josie before anyone had a chance to stand. "Mr. Gagnon, I was wondering if you could tell us about the cannibals."

Eli's eyes grew wider than before.

Charlie's mouth dropped open. "The . . . *what*?"

"Isn't there supposed to be a family of cannibals living on an island out here? Don't they sometimes come to other islands . . . you know . . . to, like, hunt people?"

"I don't know anything about that."

Bruno laughed. Too loud. "My little sister loves inventing stories."

"I didn't make it up," said Josie. "Eli told us all about it on the walk up here. Didn't he, Mom?" Vivian sat in her chair, her mouth opening and closing silently, as she searched for an answer.

Eli's parents and his sister glared at him from across the room. "Everyone back home knows the stories about these islands," he said. "I just shared one of them with Josie and Mrs. Sandoval."

Otis stood up from the couch where he'd been sitting. "And that's exactly what it is," he said, his voice quiet, sounding falsely jovial. "A story. We're all here for a good time. To celebrate Aimee and Bruno. Let's save the scary tales for later. What do you say, son?"

Eli hitched a breath. He felt like his insides were melting. "Sorry," he said, glancing at Josie. She raised an eyebrow and shrugged.

Had she done this on purpose? Tried to get him in trouble? Well, it had worked. And now he was even more annoyed than he'd been before.

So a few minutes later, while the rest of the group was following Margo and Charlie and Beatrice upstairs to the sleeping quarters, Eli snuck out the front door before his father could squirrel him away to a secluded corner and speak to him with his *real* voice, the one he used only in private.

# WAVES

# FROM THE DIARY OF
# DORY M. SAUVAGE

Saturday, August 29, 1942

Dear Diary,

You will never guess what happened! Last night, I accidentally picked up the phone and overheard Francois talking to his roommate about a secret trip they're making to Savage Island on Labor Day weekend. Only a few days from now! It's to be just the two of them and their girlfriends, Esther Acker and Betty Bellamy. Supposedly, the boys are planning to take my father's Chris-Craft out of the Haggspoint marina and return it before anyone finds out.

Can you believe the nerve of my brother? The island house has been closed up since the war started, so the entire staff has been attending to my parents at the mainland house. They'll be all alone out there. Who knows what kind of trouble they'll get into?

<u>I cannot believe they didn't invite me!</u>

Granted, I'm leaving shortly for Miss Ligustrum's School for the start of my ninth-grade year, but it would have been easy enough to take a train from Boston. They could have picked me up at a station somewhere along the way. I suppose I've finally reached an age when Frankie no longer views his baby sister as a precocious and amusing pet. Should this make me sad?

On the phone it sounded like the whole thing was Emil's idea. That boy's a troublemaker, but oh, how I adore him! His blue eyes are like sapphires. And the way his hair sometimes flops over his forehead drives my heart like a locomotive. His accent is to die for. Is there any language more beautiful than French? Enchanté! He's come to visit a couple times this summer. Who knows when I'll see him again?

Wouldn't it be a hoot if I found a way to tag along? I'd have to convince my roommate, Hilary, to cover for me with Miss Ligustrum for a few days, but I can't imagine it being a serious issue. If I could make it to Haggspoint before my brother, I may be able to sneak into the storage compartment on Daddy's boat and hide there until we get to the island. Then I'd jump out and force Frankie to deal with me!

Or, even better, what if I were to keep myself hidden when we reach the house? Play a few tricks on them as punishment before finally revealing myself? Oh boy, I'd love to see the looks on their faces.

My dearest diary, I must leave you for now. I have some planning to do.

Sincerely yours,
Dory M. Sauvage

# CHAPTER SEVEN

JOSIE REGRETTED SAYING IT the moment the words escaped her mouth: the thing about the cannibal family, blaming it on Eli. She'd realized just how cruel she'd been when she looked into his wide, worried eyes. But Eli's mother, that snooty Cynthia woman, had to understand that her little joke about the two of them falling for each other, *and getting married in a decade*, was not going to fly. Weren't they supposed to be family now? Yuck.

Upstairs, nearly a half hour after the incident, Josie flopped down on the queen-size bed in the big room that Margo, the wedding planner, had reserved "especially for her."

She'd never imagined herself falling in love or getting married, particularly not like this, on an (ooh-la-la) island, where it was supposed to be beautiful and romantic and memorable. Maybe one day, in her own way, she'd find a person she wanted to be with, but she wasn't buying this *fairy-tale-princess dream* that everyone was always trying to shove down her throat.

And how *gross* was it that her own brother was supposed to be the prince here? Did Aimee know how often he farted? Loud. Like, right in public. And they smelled worse than the hallway outside the boys' locker room after gym class. Did Aimee really understand what she'd gotten herself into? Or did she not care? Maybe Aimee farted *even worse*.

The hardest part for Josie was remembering how much she'd loved Bruno's first girlfriend, Penny D'Agostino. Bruno had started dating Penny their freshman year of high school, when Josie was only five years old. For years, their afternoons had been filled with silly television and unending packages of Twizzlers and Skittles. Penny had been funny, cracking jokes about Bruno that made him blush, which made everyone laugh even harder. Sometimes, she'd ask to hear Josie's secrets, promising to keep them locked in her heart, listening in a way that no one else bothered to do, just like a *real* big sister, the sister Josie'd never had. The sister Aimee could never hope to be. Josie had never felt closer to Bruno than when he and Penny were together.

So when Penny broke up with Bruno during their first year at college, Josie had felt her own nine-year-old heart break. She'd never felt so helpless. She'd always imagined that things would simply continue forever. Afterward, Penny would send her an occasional message, but she'd obviously moved on. She had a new life now.

If Josie had ever pictured herself at her brother's wedding, it wouldn't have been any place like this island. And it wouldn't have been Aimee by his side. Now, here they all were. Aimee had gotten what she wanted and had convinced Bruno that it was what he wanted too.

*Good luck to the both of them*, Josie thought, shoving her face into one of the fluffy down pillows to contain a brief frustrated scream.

A gust of wind came in through the open window, rustling the gauzy curtains. They reached far into the room and brushed against Josie's feet, which were dangling at the edge of the bed. She twisted around and sat up, thinking that someone had snuck in on her. But the wind came again, harder this time, catching on the pine branches just down the hill nearer to the shore and playing a single note like a harmonica. *Hmm.*

Josie felt a chill as the beam of sunlight across the wood floor disappeared. She dragged herself off the mattress and leaned on the windowsill. To her surprise, the sky was no longer the shining blue it had been when the ferry had dropped them off. Now, it was blanketed in a solemn gray from one end of the island to the other. Off in the distance, over the water, the atmosphere looked even more menacing. Darker clouds lingered there, like a monster watching the island, waiting for the perfect moment to attack. Weird. Everyone had been saying how flawless the weather was supposed to be this weekend.

Aimee would not be happy. And if Aimee wasn't happy, Bruno wouldn't be either. Josie's future sister-in-law had come to visit the Sandovals only a few times, when she and Bruno had been on break from college, but it had been enough for Josie to get a sense of her. She seemed nice on the surface, but anyone who spent a little time with her would see that Aimee always expected to get whatever she wanted. Aimee was the type who wished she could control the weather. Unfortunately, now Bruno believed it was up to him to grant that wish. Any wish as long as it kept his *love* happy.

Josie saw someone walking on the spit of land that reached out from the other side of the island. The figure was wearing Eli's blue jacket. His dirty-blond hair was cropped short, like Eli's, and he looked to be Eli's height, a bit taller than her. But hadn't Eli come upstairs to find his sleeping quarters with everyone else?

Apparently not.

She felt a tingling in her fingertips. Guilt. Would she have ever treated Bruno the way she'd been treating Eli that morning?

The island was larger than she'd first thought. Her view from here was of the yard off the side of the house and of the land opposite the wharf where they'd docked that morning. The particular stretch where Eli was hiking reached from the house, like a clam's foot, for hundreds of yards. The center of the spit was knitted tightly with pine trees. On either side were sharp rocks and steep drops to the water. Past the woods, the land was rocky and barren.

There must have been a path through the trees, because Eli had already marched beyond the grove and was heading toward the raised clearing at the land's end.

There was another building out there — the ruins of a building. Its dilapidated stone edifice rose about twenty feet from the ground. Its top was jagged where the roof had fallen in. A couple of holes in the upper part of the wall — windows maybe? — opened on the churning gray sky beyond.

What was that place? Another mansion? A forgotten guest-house? Some sort of tower? Trudging steadily forward, Eli appeared determined to reach it.

Josie suddenly felt even worse for what she'd said downstairs. If she hadn't been such a brat, maybe he'd have asked her to come with him.

The bedroom door opened behind her and then slammed shut.

Josie yelped and then turned to see which of the wedding party had decided to disturb her — her mother, maybe, or Margo, the wedding planner, butting in again where she wasn't wanted. To Josie's surprise, she discovered a girl she'd never seen before, pressing her body against the door.

The girl's chest heaved as if she'd been sprinting. Her dress was wet and covered in mud, its fabric clinging to the girl's thin frame. If Josie didn't know any better, she'd think that the girl had just been caught in a downpour. Or had crawled out of a swamp. The girl clutched at the doorknob behind herself, as if to keep someone out . . . someone who might have been chasing her.

# CHAPTER EIGHT

"WHO ARE YOU?" Josie asked.

The girl did not answer. Instead, she shut her eyes. She moved her lips, as if praying silently to herself. Her dark bobbed hair was plastered against her skull. The girl's porcelain skin gleamed between smears of grime. She looked like she might be Josie's age, if not a year or two older.

"Are you hurt?"

The girl didn't move. Josie clutched at the window frame behind her. The longer she watched this strange girl standing there, just breathing, the tighter her own lungs began to feel.

"I don't mean to be rude, but, uh, this is supposed to be my room."

The girl's eyes snapped open. She didn't seem to notice Josie — her gaze peering inward, her mind tumbling in thought. She turned around and pressed her hands against the white-painted wood door, staring at the floor now.

"Listen, if you're going to be sick . . ."

The girl glanced over her shoulder toward a door directly to Josie's left. The closet. She dashed across the room, grappled with the doorknob, then swung the door open. Josie leaped out of the way. The girl swiveled into the closet, closing the door, the latch clicking quietly behind her.

A gust of wind slammed into Josie's side, sending her scuttling into the safety of the center of the bedroom, where she could see every wall, every window, every door. She stood there for several seconds, now trying to catch her own breath. At any moment, the girl might explode out from the closet and rush at her, arms out-stretched, fingers spread wide to catch her by the shirt and drag her into the dark.

She was tempted to shout out to her mom, or anyone, for help, but a needling worry told her to keep her mouth shut. Staring at the closet door, Josie was confused more than anything else. Charlie and Beatrice Gagnon had claimed that they were alone on the island until the ferry had arrived that morning. If that was true, where had this girl come from? And why was she acting like a lunatic?

Josie felt a sharp pain in her gut as she remembered Eli's claim that there was a cannibal family out on these islands. She knew it was ridiculous to consider that maybe this girl was a member of it, but the girl certainly looked like she could be feral. Or *something*. There had been a glint of madness in her eyes, as if she'd seen something very bad, something no one should ever have seen, and as a result, her rational mind had flicked off.

Then Josie had another thought. Maybe she wasn't one of the cannibals. Maybe she was trying to get away from them! She glanced at the hall door with a sudden desire to barricade herself inside by moving the great wooden dresser a few feet to the left.

Josie hugged herself instead.

*There are no cannibals! Eli's dad had said so . . .*

*Of course* an adult *would say so . . . But that . . . that doesn't mean it's true.*

Stepping toward the closet, she sighed. She couldn't just leave the girl alone. "Who are you running from?" she asked. *Do they have forks and knives?* her brain whispered. *Spoons? Do they have a bubbling cauldron to boil our flesh?* "Is there something I can do?" she said, blinking the bloody horrors from her mind. Then, she was at the door, her ear pressed against the wood.

She felt her mouth twist into a smirk. She glanced over her shoulder at the bedroom door. This had to be some kind of joke.

"Bruno!" she called out. She ran out to the hall, peering in both directions. The other guests had left their own doors open, and pale daylight now filtered into what had earlier been a long shadowy space. "Get your butt over here!" She wandered across the hall, peering into the room where he'd left his luggage. "Bruno?"

But he didn't answer. No one answered. Quiet voices, somewhere distant, revealed that everyone must have already gone back downstairs or outside, somewhere away from here. Her smirk fell away, and she knew. This had been no joke. She was *alone* . . . except for the girl.

She retreated into her bedroom and returned to the closet door. Trembling, Josie reached for the doorknob. It was ice-cold. She turned it slowly until it wouldn't turn anymore. "Here I come," she said, a soft warning. "I won't hurt you." *And don't you hurt me either.* She pulled on the knob, feeling a slight vacuum, as if the space inside had somehow sealed itself up.

Stale air swirled out of the crack, like a rotten belch, directly into Josie's face. She coughed and then gagged. The stench smelled of mold and mildew, spores and fungus — all sorts of things that people are allergic to.

Josie stepped back, allowing the daylight to filter into the dark space. She squinted, expecting to find the girl hunched over way back in the shadows or curled into a ball on the floor. But, except for a thin layer of dust on every surface, the closet was empty.

The floor extended several feet inside. A wooden clothes rack was fastened just underneath a shelf. As Josie ducked inside, her spine shrunk, her ribs curled inward, her skin toughened like protective armor; at least that's how it felt. Reaching out, she pressed her hands against the rear wall, almost expecting it to vanish like a magic trick. But it was as solid as the rest of the closet.

The girl was gone.

Josie stumbled backward into the light of the bedroom. The wind teased the curtains again, blowing them at her like arms made of mist.

She hadn't imagined the whole thing, had she? No. There *had* been a girl.

She had obviously left the closet while Josie'd gone looking for Bruno. So where was she now?

Josie felt her spine stiffen as she imagined a hand reaching out from under the bed and grabbing her ankle. She immediately hopped several feet away from the white, frilly bed skirt. Bending over, she lifted the fabric cautiously and peered into the shadows. The space was empty, nothing but a dusty wood floor and the sagging ribs of an ancient bed frame. She glanced at the door again and then sighed, confused. Would the girl have had time to sprint down the hall while Josie'd gone looking for her brother?

There was another option. The window. Josie made her way toward the fluttering curtains, holding her breath. What would she see when she looked down? Though the room was only on the second floor, it was a significant drop.

But the grass below was clear — blowing in the breeze. Josie clutched at the window frame as a blur of blue in the distance caught her eye once again.

Eli.

# CHAPTER NINE

BY THE TIME he had made it through the trees, the wind was picking up, rustling his jacket against his body. Eli hadn't expected to walk so far, but the trail had just kept going, and his brain had been whirling so furiously that he hadn't considered stopping. Now he stood near the end of some sort of craggy, barren peninsula off the south end of the island.

Twenty yards away, on either side of him, the land disappeared — steep cliffs dropped straight down to the ocean. Behind him, by the trees, the ground had been stony earth and patchy grass, but the farther he trudged, the more it became like the layered shale at the water's edge back at the wharf — a surface so uneven it was almost threatening to twist his ankle.

Ahead, there was a crumbling stone structure — a wall of some sort, with an arched doorway — that he hadn't been able to see from back at the house. Maybe he would have noticed it if he'd been looking. But Eli had only wanted to get away.

The sky had clouded over, and the breeze came in hard again and rustled his hair. Out on the water, there were big waves now, totally unlike the glassy surface on which the ferry had glided a couple of hours ago.

One particularly strong gust moved Eli sideways, and he stumbled to the ground. A dull pain exploded from his hip and his shoulder. After a moment, he raised his hands and plucked out a few pebbles that had become embedded in his palms. He brushed off his clothes, stood up, and then glanced back toward the house.

He could just see the top floor from above the thicket of pine. For a moment, from one of the windows in the center of the building, he discerned someone watching him. A girl? Josie, maybe?

With a sigh, he turned back to the stone structure at the end of the path, hiking his blue jacket higher on his neck, as if he might be able to hide himself from her penetrating stare. A few seconds later, he crept through the doorway. Inside the structure, he sat on a large rock and caught his breath.

Several minutes passed as Eli took in the surroundings. The far wall was twenty feet tall and curved outward like a castle turret. Many slit-like openings were set inside it. He'd seen windows like this in his history textbook, in pictures of fortresses and prisons from all around the world. They were defensive features — it was easy for someone inside to aim at a target outside while remaining hidden from the enemy. The ceiling was gone. Open sky glared from above. Pieces of rotted wood stuck out from the wall several feet over his head where, Eli imagined, a second story must have once stood. Mosses and lichens covered the stone floor like a damp carpet. To his far left, a staircase descended into the ground, steps carved right into the rocky cliff. Shadows dressed the stairs in a midnight-colored camouflage.

In school, Eli had read that there were fortresses from early American wars way out in the middle of the Gulf of Maine. Maybe the building was a remnant of a famous battle. Eli stepped away from the wall, staring up, spinning slowly, imagining the possibilities of its past. People had probably died within these walls. Boats had probably been sunk in the waters just offshore. Sailors. Soldiers. People with families just like his own. Their tragic histories scattered up and down the coast, disintegrating under the pounding waves of time.

Even with the fort's ruined state, he felt protected from the wind, protected from the view of the wedding party. Grand fantasies of camping out in this fortress for the weekend began to ferment in his imagination. Fantasies of leaving the rest of the group to enjoy their party. Alone, no one could tease him or make him feel bad for wanting to be himself. Out here, he could imagine what life would be like if anyone ever actually listened to his opinion.

Someone was calling.

Eli peered around the edge of the outer doorway back toward the trees and the house on the hill. But no one was there. The sound came again, this time from behind him. Now he made out several voices. They were faint, as if shouting from far away. He couldn't discern what they were saying. The voices mixed together the way birdsong became cacophony outside his bedroom window on summer mornings.

Then, the shouting changed: A sound of terrified screaming rose up, almost indistinguishable from the howling of the wind. Eli held still, clutching his arms over his chest. He turned toward the hole in the floor, where stone steps descended into darkness. The voices cried out from below, echoing up from the shadows, like water splashing and swirling in a tidal pool. There were people down there. They were desperate for his attention.

# CHAPTER TEN

He stared down from the top step. The stairway looked solid enough, hewn from the shale itself. It followed the curved outer wall, so that from where he stood, the bottom of the stairway was not visible around an arc in the passage. Eli's throat felt constricted. Swollen. "Hello?" he called out over the drone of the wind. But the voices did not answer. Instead, there came a great pounding sound, stone on metal or vice versa. The clang reverberated up the shaft, nearly knocking Eli backward in surprise.

He took a moment to catch his breath. "Everything okay in there?" No one answered him. Eli pressed his hand against the damp stone wall as he carefully took a step down, then another. If people really were trapped, he thought, who might they be? A shipwrecked crew? Captives of the seemingly kind caretakers, the Gagnons? Eli sniffed, remembering his tale of the cannibal family. He shook his head and continued onward, the edge of the stone floor rising above his line of vision and darkening the day. At the bottom step, a tunnel stretched ahead into the shadows.

Dim light followed him as he made his way around the bend. Within a few steps, he came to a door made of black bars. Rusted hinges were bolted into the rock on the left side. On the right, an ancient chain was wrapped around a metal frame embedded into the rock, keeping the door shut.

Eli reached out to touch the chain but stopped himself. Something about this wasn't right. Was the door chained shut to keep kids like him from venturing inside? Or was it shut to keep something inside from getting out?

In the confines of the tunnel, the noise of his breathing echoed all around him, making him feel like he was surrounded by shadow versions of himself. He leaned close and listened. A hollow whirring sound came from deeper within the passage. Air moving through cracks in the rocks. Reverberations of falling water, droplets plink-plinking from a high, wet ceiling. Eli called out again: "Hello?" If there were people inside (and not just the wind and the surf, or some other anomaly of nature conjuring an auditory illusion), surely they were aware he was close by. Surely they'd answer. "Are you hurt?" He stood still and listened.

Behind the door, something was shuffling: footsteps shambling, hands grasping at walls for balance in the darkness. Eli pressed his lips together tightly, catching his breath. He stumbled backward, nearly tripping on the rising slope of shale behind him. He concentrated on the blackness beyond the door, but he could see no movement. After gathering his courage — *it's all in your mind!* — he stepped closer to the cold bars, straining to see. But inside there was only darkness.

He was about to turn back toward the stairs when he felt a warm breath on his cheek. A voice whispered to him through the gap, hushed and frightened. Eli pushed away from the door, running up the passage, pinpricks erupting across his skin, his head ringing in confusion.

"*Hilfe*," the scratch of a voice had spoken. "*Hil-fe*." The sound rippled through his head, tilting the tunnel, making him dizzy. At the stairs, Eli glanced over his shoulder, twisting his body and then catching the toes of his sneakers on the bottom step. He tripped, landing lightly on his rear. He sat for a moment, craning his head for a partial view of the door, trying to convince himself that he'd imagined it. But he knew he'd not imagined it. He could still hear the sound of it in his mind.

*Who is Hilfe?*

The door shook. The chain rattled. Something had hit the gate hard, banging it like a gong. He turned away, scrambling on his hands and knees, imagining someone crashing through the tunnel behind him, reaching out for his heels, grabbing at his sneakers, pulling him back down into the whispering pit.

Above him, the top step was a touchstone, a goal that would bring Eli back into the light. As he raced upward, he felt the rocks scraping the skin of his palms, tearing through the knees of his jeans. He slipped several times, knocking his chin once against the sharp shale.

*Bang!*

The noise sounded again, louder this time, as though the person who'd whispered to him was angry that Eli was leaving him behind. Eli squeezed his eyes shut as he continued upward, praying the rusted chain would hold.

At the top step, he swung out his arms for the nearby wall to gain a grip with which to drag himself forward. To his surprise, his hand pressed against something warm and leathery, decidedly unrocklike. It was a boot. And the boot was filled with a foot, a foot attached to a leg. As Eli glanced up, the glare of the sky overhead was a shock. It blinded him, so that he could not make out the face of the person to whom he was clinging.

# Chapter Eleven

When she laughed, Eli recognized her voice and understood. Josie had come to find him. Her eyes were wide, and her chest heaved, straining for breath.

He released her foot and struggled to lift himself to his knees. The shale floor gouged at his injuries, and he squeezed his mouth shut to keep from shouting in pain.

"I saw you from the window in my bedroom," she said, her voice wobbly. Had she run here? "What on earth are you doing?"

Eli wanted to tell her to go back to the house, to leave him alone. He worried that if he mentioned what had happened at the bottom of the stairs, she'd repeat it to everyone, embarrassing him further, daring his father to punish him in ways she probably couldn't imagine. When she extended a hand to help him up, all those bad thoughts fell away. He realized that he was actually happy she'd come to find him. Standing up fully, he said, "I'm exploring."

"Hard-core," she said, nodding at his bloody palms and scratched knees. She shoved her hands into the pockets of her purple cardigan.

"I fell."

Josie stared at him for a moment. He knew she knew he was lying . . . sort of. She reached out and touched his chin. When she pulled away, he noticed a smear of his blood on her fingertips. She bent down and wiped it on her jeans. "The caretakers probably have a first-aid kit. Patch you up."

"I'm fine," he said, ignoring the stinging sensation where she'd touched him.

She sighed and then watched him intensely for a few seconds, as if she were weighing whether to share something very important. But when she glanced at the staircase behind him, her face changed. "What's down there?"

"I-I'm not really sure."

"Isn't that where you just were?"

"Yeah, but it was, uh, really dark."

Josie smirked. "Maybe I'll go check it out myself."

"Don't!"

She flinched and then squinted at him. That intense look came over her again. "Why not? I brought my phone. There's a flashlight app. It's pretty bright." Her face was pale, and she looked nervous, as if she knew perfectly well why they should stay away from the dark passage.

"It's just . . . There's a big metal gate. And it's locked. So, there's really no point."

Josie stared down the stairs, looking more curious now than she had seconds earlier. "When I was walking here, I heard a noise. A clanging sound. Was that you?"

Eli shook his head. "I don't know who it was."

"*Who* it was? You think someone's down there?"

"Or *what* it was, I mean." He flinched. "It was probably the wind."

"It didn't sound like the wind."

"The wind can sound like a whole bunch of things other than wind." When her mouth twisted up with skepticism, Eli went on. "Voices, for example."

Josie froze for a moment, and then she glanced over her shoulder, through the ruined doorway toward the house. "You heard voices?"

"I said: *for example.*"

"What is up with you?"

"Nothing. I just got a little spooked, I guess. I didn't expect to find a ruined fort way out here on this island."

"Oh, is that what this place is? A fort?"

"I think so. Or a prison. Or something. It's pretty old. Look, you can see where it's fallen apart. The second-floor support beams there. And the ceiling . . ."

Josie glanced up and around. "It's pretty." That was not what Eli had expected her to say. "I wonder if my brother and your sister knew that a ruined building was out here when they picked this place for their wedding. Doesn't seem like something Aimee would be too happy about."

"Why do you say that?"

"I dunno. She seems . . . particular."

Eli chuckled. "You're right. She'll probably freak out when she sees this place from her bedroom window." He clutched at his throat. *"An eyesore! Ugh! Gross! Bruno, fix it!"*

Josie laughed, doubled over, clenching her stomach. She laughed so hard, it made Eli laugh too. For a moment, he almost forgot about what he'd heard down at the bottom of the stairs. When Josie caught her breath, she looked at him again, this time with concern. "Are you sure you're gonna be all right? Your chin is still bleeding."

Eli shrugged. "Does it look like it needs stitches?"

"I don't think so, but I'm obviously not a doctor."

"I think I'll live."

"Listen," said Josie. "I'm sorry about what I said earlier. In front of everyone. Your cannibal story? That was . . . kinda mean of me."

"Yeah. It was mean, I mean, but only if you did it to be mean," said Eli, smirking. "It was almost worth it to see the horrified look on my sister's face, if only for a second. And my dad was wrong, by the way. It isn't *just* a story. Everyone at my school has heard it."

"That doesn't mean it's true though, right?"

"I guess not. Lots of stories that seem like they're true actually aren't."

"And lots of stories that seem like they're lies turn out to be true," Josie said, clutching her rib cage and stepping closer to the stairwell. Something was swirling around in her head. Tidal waves. "It's hard to tell. Without evidence anyway."

"What, you're a detective now?" he asked. She didn't seem to hear him. Eli stepped toward the fort's doorway. "Let's go back to the house. Everyone's probably wondering where we are."

"Wrong," said Josie. "When I left to find you, they were all gathered in the front garden staring at the sky, jabbering on about the weather and what sort of plans they'd need to come up with in case good old Mother Nature betrays them this weekend. They barely looked at me when I passed by."

"Still," he answered, continuing to shuffle onward, hoping she'd follow, "we should be getting back."

Josie shook her head. "I don't want to."

"Why not?"

She scratched at her nose. "There's something weird about the house. I saw something. Something I don't know how to explain."

Eli wiped moisture from his forehead. He looked into her eyes, trying to see what kind of story was inside them. Was it true, or was it a lie? "What did you see?"

Josie hesitated, then answered. "I'll tell you . . . if you tell me what really happened at the bottom of these stairs."

# CHAPTER TWELVE

"*HILFE?*" JOSIE REPEATED. "You're sure that's what you heard?"

Eli nodded. "It must be a name. Don't you think? I don't know what else it could mean."

Josie shook her head. "We studied German last year. Our class only learned some basics, but I remember that word. It's one of the first things we learned." She bit her lip. "It's the German word for 'help.'"

Eli shivered. "So, you're saying that I heard someone on the other side of that door asking me to help them? *In German?*"

"Maybe."

"But who? Who could possibly be down there?"

"Maybe no one," said Josie. "Maybe it was all just the wind, like you said."

"Did something similar happen to you back at the house?"

"No," said Josie. "What I saw was completely different."

He waited for her to tell him. But she bit at the inside of her cheek and remained silent. He gritted his teeth and tried to hide his frustration by keeping his eyes wide and imploring. "We should tell someone."

"Yeah, sure. Let's go mention it to your sister."

Eli scowled. "You want everyone to think I'm making up stories again?"

Josie widened her eyes and smiled. "No," she said. "Duh. But I'm having the same trouble. I have a story *no one* will believe."

"Right," said Eli. "I told you what happened to me. Now you tell what happened to you."

"You're going to think I'm crazy," Josie answered, taking another step toward the staircase.

"But I already do."

"Har-har." She continued on down.

"What are you doing?" Eli asked, feeling a dizzy rush of panic.

"If there *is* someone down there calling for help . . . in German . . . maybe we should actually, you know, help them."

"I don't think it's a good idea. Something's not right."

"I know." She glanced back at him. "Don't you want to do something about that?"

*Not really,* thought Eli. *But if this is what it takes for you to share what you saw, then okay.*

Besides, maybe it really was the wind's fault.

He sighed, wondering how differently this conversation might have played out with Aimee instead. "Fine. You go first."

# CHAPTER THIRTEEN

THE BLACK DOOR appeared around the bend in the tunnel, looking like a portal to another dimension or time. Josie held up her phone, which was useless out here except for the flashlight beam that glowed from its back panel. "Whoa," she said, moving the light across the bars, as if examining them for rusted-out weak spots. "You're right, Eli. This *is* spooky."

To his horror, she kicked the gate. The noise erupted all around them, bouncing off the rock walls. When the echo petered out, he peeled himself away from the side of the tunnel and whispered, "Why would you do that?"

Josie ignored him. "Who's in there?" she called out. After a moment, she asked, more quietly, "Is it *you*?"

"Me?"

"No, not you."

"Then who?"

Josie shushed him, and Eli blushed. Soon, she tried again, this time, with words he didn't recognize. "*Wie gehts?*"

"Vee Gates? What's that? A name?"

"In German, it means 'How are you?' Or something like that."

"*How are you?*" Eli repeated, shaking his head. "And what if they answer, 'We're fine; thanks for asking'? Can we go then?"

"I couldn't think of anything else to say. We only studied the language for a couple months." She leaned closer to the door, listening for a response.

"You probably scared them off, knocking like that."

"Is this the chain you mentioned?" She was pointing the light at the latch. The rusted links glimmered in the pale violet glow.

"The one and only."

"There's no bolt."

Eli felt his spine lock up. His armpits had grown damp. He licked his suddenly parched lips. "But . . . Why would the person ask me for help if he could open the door himself?"

"Was there a lock the first time you came down?"

"I don't remember."

Josie reached out and began to unwind the chain from the hasp attached to the frame.

"What are you doing?!"

"I'm helping. *Helfen.* Ha-ha."

Eli stepped backward until his heels hit the bottom step of the stairwell.

"Oh, come on," Josie said. "You're not curious about what's behind the door?"

"Sure, I'm curious. It's just . . . doors are usually locked for a reason."

"True. But this one wasn't locked. It was only closed."

"My mom and dad are probably wondering where I am."

"Wrong. They're probably wondering how to calm down your sister."

The chain dangled to the ground from the gate, rattling like the tail of a snake.

Josie reached out to him, shining the light into his face. He shoved his hands in his pockets and stepped a bit closer. She shrugged, then turned and yanked the door open. Its rusted hinges squealed.

The whirring sound Eli had heard earlier whispered up the

tunnel, wrapping tenuous arms around him, a smothering hug. The noise could have been anything. Wind. Waves. Germans. The space beyond the door was pure black. He watched as Josie stepped into it a millisecond before she grabbed his wrist and pulled him along behind her.

# Chapter Fourteen

Josie shone the flashlight all around, revealing a large cavern. A few feet past the door, more steps continued down. To the right was a precipitous ledge. She and Eli took the stairs slowly, staying close to the wall on the left. The shale here was even darker, more corroded, its jagged surface slick with moisture. The salt water mixed with the odor of something fishy and rotten. Eli closed off his sinuses with the back of his tongue so he wouldn't gag.

Twenty steps down, well beyond the reach of sunlight, the stairs ended at a landing. Josie slowly swiveled her phone. The light reflected off the dampness coating the walls. Patches of a slimy substance oozed from the ceiling, looking like rotted, striped wallpaper. A few feet below, the floor was pockmarked with cracks and depressions, all filled with water. When Josie's light bounced off their sheen surface, the puddles rippled as if something living inside them had been disturbed.

"What was that?" Eli asked, squeezing Josie's hand tightly.

"Maybe little fish are trapped, like in tidal pools by the shore."

"Fish? How would they get up inside a cave?"

While remaining on the landing, Josie continued to explore the room with her flashlight, as if she might discover the answer. In the far wall, four cell-like spaces had been carved unevenly from the rock. Rusted bars grinned across the front of each. Cage doors hung askew from three of them. A fourth door lay flat inside the cell, broken entirely off its hinges.

"This cavern must have been a jail once," said Eli.

"There," said Josie, flicking her flashlight at a crevice in the floor of the farthest corner. "Listen. That's the sound of surf. This space must be connected to tunnels below. Maybe the tides force the water up to flood this room. That's how the little pools could be filled with fish and stuff."

"You're the detective here." Eli nodded. "And that was a cool science lesson, but, um, weren't we looking for a German person in need of help?"

"Do you see anyone down here besides us?"

"Well . . . no." Eli stared at the crevice in the corner. The whirring he'd heard back up at the entry seemed to be coming from there. Inside the prison cavern, the din had changed, become less focused. It spread out, bounded off the rocks, sounding less like whispering voices and more like radio static. It was the noise of a giant beast groaning in restless sleep. "But maybe he's hiding," he added. When Josie looked at him in confusion, he nodded at the dark space that was spewing the strange sounds into the fetid air.

Eyebrow cocked with the ammunition of sarcasm, Josie said, "The German begged you for help at the door up the stairs, and then climbed all the way down there?"

"Unless I was just hearing things," said Eli, his face burning. In fact, he was pretty sure that's what had happened. Now that the threat of weird German prisoners was nearly extinguished, he stepped away from Josie and off the landing.

"Don't trip," Josie warned, following him to the wet floor. "I won't be able to carry you back by myself."

"Oh, I'm sure you could if you tried really hard." Eli crept to the edge of one of the tidal pools. Josie shone the light for him. The bottom of the pool, several inches down, was covered with white blisters, living barnacles. Patches of mossy seaweed carpeted the rest of the rock. There were no fish, but a little green crab scurried out of the water, backing toward the rusted bars of the four jail cells, waving its tiny claws at them, as if to block the phone's glare. Eli bent down and stared at it for a few seconds, wondering what the crab thought about him. Nothing, probably. Just a few blips in its brain, neurons flashing DANGER.

He went on to the next pool, hoping to find something cooler.

"Don't go too far, Eli."

He stopped moving when Josie turned the light away from him, leaving him alone in the dark. She glowed at the bottom of the staircase like a ghost, the white light illuminating her face from below.

"*Okay, Mom.* You know, you were the one who wanted to come down here."

"Yeah, but only when I thought someone might have needed our help."

"You really believed that?" Eli asked. Josie sighed and rubbed at her eyes, exhausted. "A few minutes ago, when we were up at the door, you called out, *Is it* you?" He expected her to react, flinch, remember. *Something.* She only stared back. "You have an idea what's going on here, don't you?"

"I thought I did. But now . . ."

"I can't imagine all the crazy stuff that must have happened here."

"I can. You want to hear my story?"

"Finally!" He waved her forward to join him.

Josie crept across the slippery floor, avoiding the pools and the wayward green crab. Together, they sat at the edge of one of the cells, leaning against the rusted bars, while she told him about what had happened in her bedroom and how, for a moment, she'd been certain that the girl she'd seen there had somehow followed him out here.

# CHAPTER FIFTEEN

WHEN SHE FINISHED, the two sat in silence for a moment, listening to the push of the ocean through the rocks below and the plinking of water dripping from the roof of the cavern. Dim light filtered through the open door at the top of the stairs, and though their eyes had adjusted to the dark, there were still many areas of the room hidden from their view.

"You didn't think I'd follow you down here if you told me your story first," said Eli. "Right?"

Josie smiled, trailing the crab with her phone's glow. The creature crawled back down into one of the pools.

Eli squeezed his knees together. "So there really *are* other people on the island? Other than the wedding party?" He stared into the dark patches of shadow all around the space, as if one of these people were watching them right at this moment. He couldn't stop himself from standing up and taking a step toward the staircase.

"But why would the caretaker lie?" Josie stayed put, stuck in her head.

"And where did the girl go?" Eli asked. "Are you sure there wasn't some sort of secret door in the closet? The house seems like the type that might have a few of those."

"I checked. I swear. The walls were solid. I mean, maybe she slipped away when I stepped out to look for Bruno."

"And you're sure you weren't, like, dreaming? You were lying on the bed, right? Maybe you'd fallen asleep?"

"I saw her as clearly as I see you right now."

"Maybe we could see better if we went outside."

"What's the difference between what I saw and what you heard?" Josie asked, not moving.

"Well . . . I dunno. Maybe there's something about this island that messes with our senses."

Josie squinted. "Something? Like what? Magic?"

"Not magic. I mean, aren't there certain frequencies or smells or even shapes that we look at that can be disorienting? You know, *scientifically*?"

Josie snorted. "The girl in my room didn't look like a scientist."

"You know that's not what I mean."

"Let's just get out of here. My battery won't last much longer."

"My dad's going to flip if he figures out I went off by myself."

"But you're not by yourself." Josie smiled. "I'm here. I'll protect you."

"Right." Eli smiled back sadly. "From my dad? Or from the strangers on the island?"

"Whoever we run into first. Come on. If everyone's calmed down about the cloudy sky, maybe we can check in with the caretakers and ask them about this old fort."

As Josie swung her flashlight around the room one last time, Eli saw something glimmer in the corner, by the crevice where the sound of the whirring surf emanated. "Wait. What's that over there?"

"Over where?"

Eli took a deep breath and stepped lively across the floor, avoiding the pools, telling himself, *One minute more. One minute, and then we're gone.* "Would you shine your light there?" He pointed at the ground where the crevice met the wall.

Josie provided him with the light, and something in the cracked wall glinted again. Eli crouched, leaning closer to the opening.

From down in the darkness, he could make out the sound of water burbling and bubbling, washing against the hidden stones that were surely covered in the same barnacles and slime that had made their way up into the cave's shallow pools. But the sounds weren't what had his attention. In a tight gap in the side of the crack, a few inches up from where the wall met the floor, was a small piece of metal.

Josie wandered closer, providing illumination, as Eli reached out and grabbed the edge of the object. By wiggling it up and down, back and forth for a few seconds, he managed to work it loose. Soon, it fell into his palm. It was circular in shape, and though it was clearly metal, brass or copper, the sections that weren't burnished had corroded into the same dull green color as the seaweed in the pools behind them, as if the object had been trapped down in this cave for many years.

"Looks like a coin," said Josie, standing over Eli's shoulder. "Maybe it's worth something?"

"Not a coin." Eli turned the object over. "A button."

"A button? Like on a shirt?"

"Like on a coat. Or a uniform maybe. Look, you can just make out a symbol on the front." A slight indentation marked the button's surface. It looked sort of like a cross. But different.

Josie gasped. "I've seen this before. In my history class last year."

Eli's stomach squelched, as if someone had reached inside and squeezed it. "*Everybody* has seen this before. It's a swastika."

# CHAPTER SIXTEEN

ELI PINCHED THE BUTTON between his thumb and forefinger, turning it back and forth in the light. His head started to spin. Questions began to swirl inside the basin of his mind — they bubbled and overflowed. "Why?" he whispered.

"Why what?" Josie asked.

"Why is it down here?" He glanced back at Josie. "Who did it belong to? What happened in this place?"

"Nazis?" Wide-eyed, Josie shook her head. She crouched down beside him on the other side of the crevice. "Can I see it?"

Eli held out the button. Josie cupped her hand underneath to catch it.

*Hilfe* . . .

Eli squeezed the button into his fist so hard that veins popped out of his forearm, little rivers of blood running under his prickled skin. "Please tell me you heard that."

Josie clenched her jaw and nodded stiffly.

*Hilfe* . . .

The voice was barely a whisper, but the word it spoke was as clear as spring water.

"It came from down there," Josie said, peering into the dark space between their feet.

A pungent odor wafted up from the crevice: a mix of sulfur, salt, and rotting garbage. Eli recognized it as the low-tide stench that was infamous at some Maine beaches. Though it was familiar, it still made him want to gag.

The door at the top of the stairs slammed shut — *Wham!* —

the hinges squealing, the chain rattling as it dragged across the floor.

Eli and Josie fell away from each other in surprise. Josie dropped her phone. It landed beside her boot, the flashlight side down, and the room went dark.

Before they could recover, or even process what had happened, a terrible noise rose up, as if from the crevice, an awful screaming, voices calling out in panic and terror. The screaming intensified, pounding painfully into their eardrums. With his mouth stretched in a wide *O*, Eli realized that his own voice was now helping create the deafening chaos.

The door at the top of the steps slammed open and shut, again and again.

*Wham! Wham! Wham!*

Josie snatched up her phone, the flash blurring Eli's vision. They both scrambled to regain their balance, but Eli's foot slipped. Reaching out to catch himself, he opened his fist and slammed it against the wet wall, dropping the button. Glancing down, he watched it turn once in the air, a flash of its horrible symbol winking at him, before dropping into the crevice.

When it was gone, the sounds stopped.

Stumbling away from the wall of the cavern, Eli ran, not thinking about where he was going, not noticing that he was still emitting a low whine from the back of his throat. Josie followed at his heels, poking at his shoulders, steering him toward the stairs.

The door was partially open, dim light spilling in from the tunnel outside. Before he knew it, he was stumbling up into overcast daylight at the top of the stairs and onto the ground level of the fort. Breathless, Josie followed right behind him.

Neither of them spoke as they raced onward through the outer doorway and onto the barren spit of land that rolled out before the woods, where the overgrown trail led back up to the house on the hill.

# WHITECAPS

# FROM THE DIARY OF
# DORY M. SAUVAGE

Friday, September 4, 1942

Dear Diary,

Everything is settled! I leave tomorrow morning by bus. Boston to Haggspoint with a single transfer in Portland. From the station, I'll walk to the marina and wait. Frankie, Emil, and the girls should be arriving in the early afternoon.

I've packed my suitcase with some of my best dresses along with a few snacks for the trip. I'm not sure what's left in the pantry out on the island. Probably preserved vegetables from the garden. Sacks of dried beans and rice. Cans of tomatoes and sauces. Maybe after I reveal myself, I'll prepare a hearty meal for everyone. I've been watching the cook, Mrs. Jackson, in our own kitchen for the past few months, and I've learned a whole lot.

I haven't told anyone other than my roommate, Hilary, that I'm doing this. I wish I could take her with me, but she agreed that without the story that she's prepared — regarding vaguely painful female troubles — Miss Ligustrum will insist that I leave our room for meals and introductions. I wonder what the other girls would think if they knew what I was about to do? Would they be jealous? Or would they think I'm crazy? I would wager that it might be a little bit of both.

Until next I write, dear Diary, I remain

Your best friend,

Dory M. Sauvage

# CHAPTER SEVENTEEN

WHEN THEY'D MADE IT halfway through the woods, they finally slowed, then stopped completely, attempting to come back into their bodies.

Eli planted his feet into the mulchy soil, placed his hands on his thighs, leaned over, and struggled to catch his breath. Blood pounded in his skull, like an alarm clock ticking away, reminding him that he was alive, that he was awake and not dreaming.

Across the trail, Josie plopped down on the moss-covered trunk of a fallen pine. With her eyes closed, she threw her face up to the canopy of pines — her long hair dangling off the back of her head, reaching nearly to the forest floor — and sighed loudly.

The two of them glanced at each other. For a mysterious reason that neither of them understood, they found themselves smiling. Quickly, their smiles transformed into grotesque exaggerations — too wide, too filled with teeth — that reflected the madness from which they'd run. This was followed by an uncontrollable fit of giggles. Eli laughed so hard that he fell backward, wetting the seat of his pants on the permadamp of the ground. This only made Josie guffaw harder. They laughed as if it would fix everything — chase away demons, or something.

A few minutes later, they grew as silent as the woods that surrounded them, their breath coming as easy now as the breeze that shook the pine needles high over their heads.

"What happened back there?" Josie asked, her eyes wide with giddiness. "What was all that?"

"The wind?" Eli said. They both giggled again.

"The wind. Ha-ha. Good one."

"I was really scared."

"I could tell!"

"But you heard it too, right? The voice that whispered that word."

Josie nodded. "*Hilfe*. Clear as day."

"What do we do now?" Eli asked.

"What do you mean?"

"Well, I can't go tell my mom and dad what we saw. What we heard. They'll think I'm trying to make trouble." He sighed. "I can't believe I dropped that button."

Josie shrugged. "You don't have to tell them anything you don't want to," she said. "After we clean ourselves up, we can ask the caretakers a little more about this place, like we planned. They've got to know something."

"I'm sure they do," Eli said, standing up and trying uselessly to brush off the moist grime that coated his rear end. "But are they willing to share?"

# CHAPTER EIGHTEEN

At the top of the hill, Eli and Josie crept to the front entrance of the house. In the foyer, Eli found his suitcase propped against the wall. From down the hall, voices of the wedding party echoed, arguing about one thing or another.

Josie led the way upstairs and stopped outside her bedroom, then pointed several doors down to where she remembered Margo Lintel had said Eli would be staying. "There's a bathroom across the hall," she said, touching her chin to remind him to clean away the blood on his own.

"Thanks," he whispered.

When he'd gone, Josie glanced into her own bedroom. She listened for a moment, trying to make out the sound of breathing or maybe a creak as someone hidden shifted his or her weight. After she was certain she was alone, she stepped inside. The clouds through the window had grown denser. Darker. The ocean in the distance was speckled with bits of white, where foam frosted the largest waves. A storm was coming, no matter what the weather people had predicted, no matter how much Aimee cried or how much Bruno tried to comfort her.

Josie thought of the girl who'd burst through her door earlier that morning. She remembered the panicked look in her eyes. If the girl had experienced the same kind of strangeness that Josie and Eli had encountered down at the fort, it was no wonder she'd seemed so out of it. Josie didn't know what she would have done if she'd been alone down in that cavern when the voices started screaming. She wondered, *What amount of fear does it take for a person to completely lose it?*

She decided to leave her bedroom and wait for Eli down in the foyer instead.

Fifteen minutes later, Eli found her sitting on the bottom step of one of the dual staircases, fiddling with her phone. Electronic beeps and blips reverberated around the white room. She was engrossed in a game and didn't hear him approach.

He grasped the banister at the balcony, certain that anything he said or did would make her jump. The alternative was to leave her alone and stay by himself in his room, but he didn't feel like doing that anymore. They were about to become family. If Eli had gone out to the spit to steer his own ship, maybe Josie's arrival meant that they were riding in the boat together now.

"Hey," he said quietly. She flinched and then whipped her head around to look at him. "Sorry!" he said. But she smirked. No harm done. "I guess you still have some battery left?"

"A bit," she said, slumping her shoulders. "I really should charge it before it dies."

Eli started down the stairs. He'd washed his face and wetted his hair. The cut on his chin was a mere nick, barely noticeable. He'd wiped the muck away and then changed his jeans. The morning had felt epic. According to the clock on the table next to his bed, it was barely noon. But Eli felt new. Fresh. Ready to find some answers to the frightening questions that they'd raised in the fort at the end of the craggy spit.

# CHAPTER NINETEEN

ELI AND JOSIE CREPT down the hallway toward the voices of their families in the rear of the house. They were in a sitting room just off the solarium, staring at a large television. Whispering static snow filled the screen.

"I don't understand," said Aimee, perched on the edge of a couch, crossing her legs tightly, waggling one anxious foot. "How could none of the reports have predicted this storm system before we left this morning? I mean, look out the darn window! It's practically nighttime out there."

"Charlie already told us, babe," Bruno said, his voice calm. "These kinds of squalls pass by all the time out here on the water. Give it an hour or so."

Across the hall from the sitting room, Eli and Josie heard a loud clattering. In the kitchen, someone was banging around pots and pans, plates and utensils.

"It doesn't matter, darling," said Cynthia, who was tucked up on an overstuffed chair situated kitty-corner to her daughter. "Margo and Gregory are working things out in the Gagnons' office. Don't you worry. They'll take care of it all."

"I just hope Carlos and his mother can still get here tomorrow," said Vivian, standing by the window. "Those waves are looking intense out there."

Bruno shot his mother a look. Vivian glanced quickly at Aimee's wan, unhappy face and then turned away, smiling.

"Now, now," said Otis, raising the remote control. "Enough

about the weather. Enough about the wedding. Let's check out the game. I bet they've got clear skies over Boston."

Aimee folded her arms and flopped back against the couch cushions. "Dad, the storm knocked out the reception. This is what we were *just* talking about."

"And the Internet?"

"Same deal," said Bruno. "Sorry, sir."

Otis grunted, stood, and moved toward the window to stare at the sky.

"We'll all feel better once we eat something," said Cynthia. "Beatrice said lunch is soon."

Aimee shook her head. "I'm so nervous, I'll probably puke if I try to eat anything."

"Come on," Eli whispered to Josie, nodding toward the kitchen. "The caretakers must be in here." The two snuck unnoticed through the doorway.

The kitchen was industrial looking. Large windows opened out on a clearing. On bright days, warm light must flood the room. Now, flickering fluorescents illuminated the steel appliances, making the place appear clinically sterile.

Beatrice Gagnon stood at a wooden island in the center of the room. She was chopping up vegetables with a large knife and then tossing them into a wide yellow ceramic bowl. At the sink behind her, Charlie was rinsing utensils. "Do we have enough mustard?" he asked over his shoulder. "If not, I'll radio Sonny to bring some along tomorrow."

"The radio's still not working, hon, but I'm sure we're just fine with our amount of mustard. I really think you overestimate people's love of that condiment." Beatrice glanced up as Eli and Josie came closer. "Oh. Hello there."

Charlie turned around, water dripping from his fingertips and splashing on the white tiled floor. "Lunch is almost ready. Salad and sandwiches. Build your own. You kids hungry?"

"Yeah," said Eli. "I could eat, like, a whole . . . head of lettuce."

Josie squinted at him quizzically and then nodded in nervous agreement. "He really likes salad."

"Good," said Beatrice, returning her knife to the celery stalk in front of her. "I'm glad to see you two have become better acquainted."

"Totally," said Josie. "We've already taken a little stroll around the island."

"Have you really?" Charlie asked. "See anything interesting?"

"You could say that," Eli answered.

Beatrice's knife rattled against the cutting board; a rapid-fire echo flitted around the room.

"We walked the trail through the woods," said Josie, "and we found that weird building up on the cliff across the island."

The caretakers both tensed before turning to look at each other. Charlie smacked his lips nervously before saying, "Yeah, it's . . . a little dangerous out there. The ground's unstable. I meant to put up a sign. *Do not enter.* Something like that." Eli and Josie examined the floor. "You went in, didn't you?"

"Oh, well, not really," said Eli. "I mean, we peeked."

Charlie knitted his brow.

"We didn't know it might be dangerous," said Josie, her voice firmer than Eli's. "But we did want to ask you about the building."

"About this house too," Eli spoke up. He expected the caretakers to have some reaction to that. But their faces remained strangely stonelike. "I mean . . . Josie and I have both experienced some weird things in the past few hours. You know, since we got off the ferry."

"Weird things?" Beatrice asked, her expression clouded. She used the edge of the knife to scoop the chopped celery into her hand and then dropped it into the bowl. "You're not still harping on those cannibalism tales, are you? Your father —"

"No, ma'am," Eli said quickly, his face flushing.

"Then, what? What *weird things*?"

Josie glanced at Eli. For a moment, neither of them spoke. They didn't know where to start.

# CHAPTER TWENTY

ELI WENT THROUGH everything that had happened down at the ruined building, admitting to exploring the strange cavern. Charlie and Beatrice listened, emotions hidden behind masks of indifference, as Eli told them about the frightening sounds, the slamming door, the rattling chain, and the disembodied whisper of the word *Hilfe*. Josie chimed in, providing a translation in case they needed it. Finally, Eli mentioned the corroded button he'd pulled from the edge of the deep crevice in the corner of the cavern. He even told them about the wicked symbol that decorated it.

At this, the couple's eyes finally went wide. "And you still have this button?" Beatrice asked.

Eli's gaze fell to the floor. "Well, no. In all the commotion, I dropped it. It fell into the crevice."

"Shame," said Charlie, almost wistfully. "I would have liked to have seen —"

"The island has quite a history," Beatrice interrupted. "Much of it remains a mystery. At least to the two of us."

"But you've lived here for so long," said Josie. "You must know *something*."

Beatrice bit at the inside of her cheek for a moment, then clicked her tongue against the roof of her mouth. "I can tell you that the building you stumbled upon is an old fort from the time of the American Revolution," she said wearily, as if this was a story she'd shared more times than she cared to remember. "That much I know is true. I can also tell you that when the wind picks up and you're standing inside those walls, you might feel like God himself is talking to you."

"God?"

Beatrice smiled. "Let's just say, I've heard strange things down there too. And though at first I convinced myself otherwise, I'm certain now that all it's ever been is the wind blowing through the nooks and crannies of what's left of that structure."

"We thought it was the wind too, at first," Eli said.

"What else could it have been?"

The four stared at one another in silence for a moment. Though he had a few theories, Eli kept his mouth shut.

"And the wailing?" Josie asked.

Charlie laughed. "You're from New York City, aren't you?"

Josie nodded. "Staten Island."

"Then you probably haven't heard a herd of seals barking to one another, have you?"

"Seals?" Josie shook her head, confused.

"We've got quite a few of 'em in these waters. They eat our fish and bask on the rocks at low tide. I'll bet you a million smackers that what you heard was some sort of mating call. That or a great big fight between a couple of the alpha boys. Their cries can echo up through the sea caves below the fort."

"Seals," Eli said to himself, trying to remember the feeling he'd gotten down there in the darkness. Could the answer have been as simple as that? Could the wind whipping through that tunnel have slammed that door open and closed so madly? "But it sounded so much more . . ." More what? Terrifying? Dangerous? He changed direction. "The fort. It was built by Americans?"

"That's what they say," Charlie answered.

"Any chance people used the fort later on?"

"Later on?"

"It's just . . . That button I found. I thought maybe the Germans could have landed here. Maybe the Americans used the fort during World War II?"

"Well, if they did, you won't find it in any history book," said Charlie. "I remember reading that the East Coast was on high alert for the possibility of an attack. In fact, I believe some U-boats were spotted off the coast of New Jersey. Fired on a tanker. Isn't that right?" He glanced at Beatrice. She shrugged. "I think the US naval fleet was stationed around the islands off Portland, to our west. The defenses there were high. But out here . . ." Charlie sniffed. "What would anyone have wanted with old Stone's Throw?"

Eli sighed. He'd been totally convinced that the button with the symbol on it had been connected to the German word spoken by that strange voice. *Hilfe.* The amused look on the caretakers' faces told him that he'd been wrong. However the button had gotten into the cave, it must have been a coincidence.

Josie took a deep breath and then released it slowly. "Mr. Gagnon," she said, "down at the wharf we heard you say that you and your wife were the only ones on the island this morning."

Eli glanced at Josie, his heart suddenly pounding. He'd almost forgotten that there'd been more than one big question they needed answered.

Charlie crossed his arms and leaned back against the sink. "That's right."

Josie licked her lips and swallowed something dry down her throat. "When I was lying on the bed in my room earlier, a girl came through the door."

Beatrice turned quickly to look at her husband. Charlie's eyes flashed. Anger? Embarrassment?

But the caretakers remained silent, and Josie went on. "She had short brown hair, and she was wearing this soaking wet dress.

Peach colored. Stained with mud. She might have been a couple years older than Eli and me. She wouldn't answer when I asked her who she was or if she was okay. She only stood there silently for a moment and then dashed into the closet. When I opened the door to look in on her later, she was gone."

"Charlie," said Beatrice, "there was no one else on Sonny's boat this morning, was there?"

"Nope," said Charlie. "As far as I know, just the seven from the family. Plus Margo and Gregory."

Beatrice glanced at Josie, a bemused look smeared like a smile across her jaw. "Well, that sounds . . . impossible. There's no girl in this house. Other than you, my dear."

"But I saw her," said Josie. "She wasn't like the . . . the wind down at the fort. She was actually there."

"Then where did she go?" Charlie asked, turning back to the sink, flipping the faucet back on. Water rushed from the pipes and splashed into the basin, filling the kitchen with white noise.

"That's what I was hoping you might know."

"I haven't noticed a mud-covered girl running around this house," he said. "Have you, Beatrice?"

"I . . ." Beatrice began, but when Charlie flicked water from his fingers at her, she jumped. Then she snickered nervously. "No, of course not." She cocked her head and said, "You say you were lying down, Jodie? Maybe it was a waking dream. I've had that happen to me before."

"My name is *Josie*," she answered firmly. "Josephine, actually. And it wasn't a dream. I'm sure of it."

Beatrice grasped the handle of the knife tightly. "If there were someone else on this island, just who do you imagine it would be?" Josie blinked at the woman, totally shut down by her change in tone. "Really. I'd like to know your thoughts. *Who is this girl?*" Eli watched Josie bite her lip. Silence thrummed in the room. Beatrice squinted at them and lowered her voice. "Maybe my husband and I have a secret daughter whom we cannot control." Eli couldn't tell if she was teasing or not. "Maybe she escaped from the fortress where we've been keeping her prisoner." The woman raised an eyebrow, sharp as a blade. "Maybe the girl is starving and she's spent the morning sorting out which of you might make the best meal." She slammed the tip of the knife into the cutting board and smiled as Josie and Eli flinched. "What's wrong? Aren't these the answers you're imagining? Isn't this what you wanted to hear?"

Eli held his breath. He hadn't expected the conversation to take this turn. "Maybe we should go." He hooked Josie's arm with his own and pulled her toward the door behind them.

"Wait." When the two turned back to the caretakers, they were surprised to find Beatrice's face red, looking almost regretful. "I'm sorry," she said, her breath heavy. "It's just . . . My husband and I only want everyone here to have a lovely weekend. Isn't that right, Charlie?" Despite the lift at the sides of the older woman's mouth, now there was a hardness in her eyes. "No more questions, okay?" She turned her gaze to the space behind them. "Besides, you wouldn't want to upset your parents, would you, Eli?"

A pair of heavy hands fell on Eli's shoulders. "Upset your parents?" said his father, before spinning him around. Eli looked up. Otis glared down at him. "Upset us how?"

"Oh, it's nothing!" Beatrice called out, full of celebration and cheer. "We were just chatting about our house's mysterious history. You've got a couple of sleuths in your party, Mr. Barker."

Otis's eyelids slivered, and Eli tried to shrink away. His father clenched harder at his shoulders. "What have you been up to?"

"Please, Mr. Barker," said Beatrice, louder this time, more chipper. "Eli's done nothing wrong. I was just . . . *telling stories.*" She glanced between Josie and Eli, wearing a knowing look, a silent alarm of warning. "Now, would you all do me a favor and ask the group to join us in the dining room? Lunch is just about ready."

Otis stared at Eli for a few more seconds. If he noticed the nick on Eli's chin, he didn't mention it. Then he smiled at Beatrice. "No problem. Everyone is real hungry."

# CHAPTER TWENTY-ONE

THE MEAL WAS a light, casual affair. The group grabbed plates of food from the dining room table and then sectioned off, wandering around the ground floor of the house, examining the myriad artworks hanging on the walls and taking in the views of the blustering ocean through the towering windows.

Eli and Josie made their way outside to the front garden. They sat in the grass near the fountain, eating in silence as the breeze rustled the purple flowers around them. Every time Eli swallowed a bite of his sandwich, he fought to keep it down. A lump kept coming back up, and his eyes stung. But he would not cry in front of Josie. He wouldn't cry *at all*, not even alone, not this weekend, if he could help it.

"Your dad's kind of scary," Josie said after a few minutes, as if reading his mind.

Eli picked at his teeth, pretending he didn't hear. "What do you think the caretakers were up to back there?"

"Making lunch?"

He shook his head. "They're hiding something. Obviously."

Josie stared at the grass between her boots and shrugged.

"Did you not notice she was trying to terrify us?" Eli prodded.

"Oh, I noticed. Do you think maybe there was some truth about the girl being their daughter?"

"I don't know," said Eli, wishing he could force away the blush from his cheeks.

Josie waved her hands, as if to change the conversation. "We're only here for a few days. This is nothing to get worked up about."

To Eli, the possibility of a strange girl who no one wanted to talk about entering Josie's room without her permission actually *did* seem like something to get worked up about. He lowered his head and plucked at the lawn. "I just didn't like the way that lady talked to me is all."

Josie sighed. "Maybe we should forget about all this stuff for now. Who knows? Maybe it *was* all just wind and seals and dreams."

They talked about other things. Josie told Eli about her friend Lisa, about the races they had held during afternoons over the summer: one at a time around the block, clocking in faster and faster as the weeks went by. How afterward, they'd reward themselves with vanilla soft-serve cones from the McDonald's on the corner. Eli shared the tale of his graphic novel, the one he was writing with Shane Mullins, about the invisible dolphin with supersonic psychic abilities that lives in a grimy aboveground pool behind an abandoned house in Florida and solves mysteries with the only three human kids in the neighborhood who know she exists. Josie laughed, but in a good way, as if she understood that it was supposed to be silly. It was nice. When he'd mentioned the project to Aimee, she'd rolled her eyes and scoffed.

"How'd you come up with that?" Josie asked.

"Sleepovers at Shane's house. Late at night we get into giggling fits. I guess we were trying to one-up each other with the most ridiculous ideas that popped into our heads. That one stuck. I dunno why."

"I can't wait to read it."

"It'll be a while," said Eli, slumping his shoulders. "Neither of us can draw."

"But won't that make it even funnier?" Josie smiled. "This crazy story with terrible illustrations? I think you guys could work it out."

"Thanks," said Eli. "That . . . means a lot. We're gonna try this fall. For real. We've got big plans."

"I think it's cool to be passionate about something you're doing just for yourself. Not for a teacher. Not for your parents. Just for you. You and your friend. No matter what it is. A graphic novel. Singing in the shower. Running around the block as fast as you can."

Eli nodded, realizing that the lump had gone from his esophagus. His eyes were wide and clear. Empty of that stinging sensation he'd felt when he'd first sat down in the grass.

"Yeah. So I guess we're both pretty cool, right?" he said, wrinkling his nose, pulling up his upper lip into a grotesque face that he usually reserved for his time alone with Shane.

Thankfully, Josie laughed again. "Oh, good," she said, as if to herself. "My new brother-in-law is an idiot."

"*Brother-in-law!*" he said and then broke into giggles.

Behind them, the front door squealed as it opened. Otis stepped out onto the marble landing. It took a moment for him to notice them sitting by the fountain.

Eli shrunk back, as if he might be able to hide. Then, to his surprise, Otis waved. "Going fishing," Otis called out. "You two want in?"

Bruno and Aimee appeared in the doorway behind him. Aimee held two fishing poles and a bag filled with leftover bread from lunch. Bait. Bruno carried a small plastic tackle box. Charlie must have given them supplies.

"Not really," Eli said, loud enough only for Josie to hear.

Josie ignored him. Standing, she tugged his wrist. "Come on. It'll be a good distraction. For *everyone*."

Eli looked out at the water. The waves were coming in heavy and harsh now. Surf splashed high above the wharf. He'd be surprised if any of them caught seaweed, never mind a fish.

# Chapter Twenty-Two

THE CARETAKERS' APARTMENT was a trio of small rooms just off the kitchen, separate from the grandeur of the mansion, sparsely furnished but elegant in its simplicity.

Standing by the cupola window in the den, Margo Lintel worried about the possibility of rain. Every bride wished for fair skies. But Margo was fearful of much more than the weather's effect on the wedding.

Gregory Elliott bent over a rickety wooden desk, on top of which sat a shortwave radio. He fiddled with its knobs, searching for any working frequency. Currently, the old speaker was only emitting brief bursts of static.

For a moment, Margo imagined that life here must be pleasant, free from the stresses of the mainland, but then she recalled the surreal experiences she'd had since arriving on the island, and she knew, without doubt, that she would not last one night alone on Stone's Throw Island. "Anything yet?" she asked Gregory, trying to swallow the nervous squeak in her voice back down into her chest.

"Unfortunately, no. Maybe there's something wrong with the radio. Or maybe it's on Sonny's end. When Charlie finishes cleaning up lunch, I'll ask him to come in and take a look at it."

"Wonderful. Thank you, Gregory." From the window, Margo glimpsed the woods and part of the grassy slope that led down to the wharf.

As the winds rose, the clouds dashed from one horizon to the other. This only added to the strange feeling she hadn't been able

to shake since before stepping off Sonny's ferry that morning —
the feeling caused by the men she'd seen watching her from shore.
Then there was the girl who'd disappeared into one of the bedrooms upstairs when Margo'd first gone up to prep the sleeping
arrangements. She'd checked the room but found it empty.

She felt like she hadn't been getting enough sleep, but she
couldn't very well lie down right now and take a nap. What
she could do, however, was try to get in touch with her own family.
But in order to do that, she'd have to get through to Sonny.

Months earlier, when Margo told her brother about the wedding out on Stone's Throw, he was surprised. Robert was familiar
with many of the islands off Haggspoint, but Stone's Throw was
not one of them.

After the recent sale, rumors spread that fishermen had
encountered strange equipment in the waters nearby — corroded
contraptions that looked like some sort of old-fashioned surveil-
lance gear attached to buoys with thick, barnacle-crusted cables
that dropped deep into the churning gulf. They had hinted that
the government might have once carried out secret tests in the old
mansion during the early days of the Cold War. Margo dismissed
these tales as no more believable than the local legends she'd grown
up with.

But she could not dismiss what she was currently feeling:
desperation. Robert needed to know that a storm was heading
his way.

Ever since she could remember, their mother, Thea, had had a
phobia of thunderstorms. Though Thea lived in an elder-care
home miles inland from Haggspoint, Robert would need to be
with her, to distract her, lest she throw a fit and hurt herself. If
Thea had known that Margo was out in the gulf, on a secluded
island no less, Robert would have asked the aides to sedate her;
however, the only thing that Margo had mentioned to her was she

was working a wedding over the weekend and that she'd be back on Monday night.

"Darn it," said Gregory, still concentrating on the radio. "Almost had something. Did you hear that? A voice?"

"No," said Margo, staring out the window, as if lost in a dream. "I missed it."

Outside, the two children, brother and sister of the bride and groom, stood on the wharf beyond the boathouse with some of the adults, throwing fishing lines out into the turbulent surf. She felt a pang, remembering how she and Robert had once played along the coastline, on Sundays when their father had been alive. Margo watched, enthralled as the girl struggled to reel in what looked like a ten-pound something-or-other.

Margo touched the glass and released a soft gasp. The object Josie had pulled up was a large black boot, tall and decayed, dripping with yellow tendrils of weed. The group at the wharf laughed when she dropped the boot onto the deck. Margo, however, felt sick. Though she couldn't quite make out details, it looked like it might have been the same type of boot the men had been wearing as they'd watched the ferry approach the island earlier that morning — the men whom Charlie insisted did not exist.

# THE SQUALL

# FROM THE DIARY OF
# DORY M. SAUVAGE

Saturday, September 5, 1942

Dear Diary,

I made it to the island without being discovered!

Currently, I am sitting in my secret room, writing to you by candlelight. Outside, it has started to storm, hopefully just a passing squall. The sound of the rain on the roof is making me sleepy. But I cannot sleep. Not yet! I haven't even begun the sabotage of Frankie's party.

I spent the afternoon and the evening around the house and the yard in various hiding spots, listening in on their conversations, and I've learned a few things about my brother that I can certainly use as collateral the next time he decides to leave me out of his plans. And I thought that his roommate, Emil, was the troublemaker of the two! This has been so exciting. I feel like one of those undercover agents in Europe who you see in the newsreels at the movies!

Just after the sun had set, when I was out back by the trees collecting muddy stones, I did notice something odd. I'm not sure what to make of it. Emil appeared in one of the bedroom windows upstairs. He stood staring out at the ocean. In one hand, he held up a kerosene lantern that he must have brought onto the island, because I certainly don't remember my father having anything like that here. With his other hand, Emil was waving his palm before the flame, up and down, in a strange pattern. It made me a little nervous to see him doing this — Daddy spent an entire evening with the family at the beginning of the summer warning Mama and the staff why villages up and down the East Coast must keep lights off after sunset. We don't want to become targets of the enemy. And any light in the darkness can be revealing.

I'll have to mention this to Emil once I expose my presence. I wouldn't want him to make that mistake again.

More soon...

Your friend,

Dory M. Sauvage

# Chapter Twenty-Three

No one caught a fish. But everyone was having so much fun, it didn't matter.

By the time Josie had dragged the boot up from the choppy water, the small group was too giddy to focus anymore. Minutes later, a gust of wind whipped down the hill from the house, shaking the pine branches furiously, and barreled into Eli, pushing him precariously close to the edge of the wharf. After that, Otis decided it was time to call it quits. Even Aimee, who'd cast her reel with such intensity as if to beat Mother Nature at her game, reluctantly conceded that it was best to bring the party back inside. As soon as she and Bruno stepped onto the path up to the house, rain began to fall.

Josie and Eli raced ahead, clutching their lunch plates, happy they'd gone fishing with Bruno and Aimee and Otis instead of hiding away as they'd done for most of the morning.

Once inside, they stopped off in the kitchen and placed the plates in the dishwasher.

"I've got to charge my phone for a few minutes," said Josie. "We can hang out in my room, if you want."

But when they reached the top of the stairs, a peach-colored blur flew past them down the hallway, shocking the two into silence. Josie and Eli froze where they stood, watching as a girl stopped before Josie's bedroom door. The girl swung the door inward and disappeared inside.

"That's her!" said Josie, dashing off in the same direction.

Eli followed. "The girl?"

"Yes, the girl! She's back."

Josie grappled with the doorknob. It wouldn't turn, as if someone on the other side was holding it in place. "Hey!" Josie called out. "We need to talk to you!"

Josie cranked her wrist to the right and the knob gave way, but when she pushed on the door, it held tight. She felt the girl pressing back and remembered her experience earlier that morning — the way the girl had burst through the door and then leaned against it, as if to keep someone out. The same thing was happening again here, as if someone had rewound time and pressed play, only now, Josie was seeing the film from another angle. Soon, the pressure lessened, and Josie's weight carried the door inward. Falling across the threshold, she caught a glimpse of the closet door slamming shut. The girl had once again escaped into the sequestered shadows.

Eli slipped past Josie and into the room. He raced to the closet door and yanked it open. "Wait!" Josie called out, worried that the girl might pounce on him.

But when Josie saw Eli's confused expression, she understood immediately — the girl wasn't there.

# CHAPTER TWENTY-FOUR

WIND RUSHED THROUGH the open window, whipping the gauzy curtains. Droplets of rain splattered through the screen onto the wood floor. The breeze caught the bedroom door and slammed it shut behind them. Surprised, Josie and Eli stumbled away from the closet and toward the end of the big bed as if the safest place in the room might just be underneath it.

After a minute, Josie broke toward the window, slipping slightly on the wet floor, and drew down the sash. The curtains fell flat. But the wind thrashed rain at the old, rippled glass, rattling several loose panes and declaring the storm's frenzied arrival.

She turned her attention back to the closet door. "You saw her, right?" Josie asked. "We *both* saw her."

Eli nodded. The frightened, electric feeling that had buzzed his bones at the fort that morning was back. His fingertips prickled, and he fought to slow his breath.

Josie shook her head. "So where is she now?" She waved her arms up and down to indicate the empty closet.

Eli approached it again. Standing in the doorway, he observed solid white surfaces. There was a sharp simplicity to the space. He allowed himself to imagine the impossibility of a girl disappearing into it like a magician's apprentice into a box on a stage — but there was always a trick to those shows, some sort of secret that the audience never learned.

Though the window was closed, he shivered as if another gust rushed the room. He turned to face Josie. "She was covered in mud and dirt. Right?"

"I was able to catch a better glimpse the first time she ran through," she answered, "but yes, she was filthy. Her dress was practically plastered to her body." Eli nodded at the bedroom door. It was painted bone-white. He pointed at the closet's crystal doorknob. Josie squinted at him, confused. Then, her lips parted. She drew a small breath. "No handprints. No dirt."

"So she cleaned up after herself?"

Josie didn't know what to think. She sat on the mattress and drew her knees to her chest.

Eli stepped toward her, but when she flinched, he kept his distance. "Josie," he said, struggling to keep his voice steady, "do you believe in ghosts?"

She sneered. "As opposed to cannibals?"

Eli tried to smile but ended up grimacing awkwardly. "Forget about cannibals," he said, then shook his head. "Do you believe that places can be haunted?"

"I don't know. I never thought seriously about it before." Josie stared into the open closet. Her vision blurred and she could almost see the figure of the girl staring back out at her. She closed her eyes. "But, yeah, I guess I could believe that this house is haunted."

"Okay, that's a start. But what if it's not just the house?" said Eli, settling onto the mattress several feet from her. He nodded toward the window. Josie turned and looked at the ruins in the distance. "What if it's the whole island?"

# CHAPTER TWENTY-FIVE

JOSIE SLID OFF the bed with a groan and landed on the floor with a hearty thump. She tapped the edge of the closet door tentatively with her toe, and the door swung shut. Distracted, she pulled her phone out of her pocket and strolled around to the other side of the bed, where she'd left her duffel bag. She rifled through one of its compartments until she located her charger, then she plugged her phone into the outlet at the baseboard behind the bedside table.

Eli watched, confused. "No thoughts on the matter?"

Josie stood up straight and stared into his eyes. "You're suggesting that the voices we heard at the fort weren't barking seals. And the girl who keeps sneaking into my bedroom isn't a member — or a victim — of a cannibalistic family. The answer is as simple as . . . *ghosts*." She crossed her arms. "Great. So what?"

"So what?"

"Yeah, *so what?* You want to go talk to the Gagnons again? Or maybe your dad? You think that'll help? You think you're going to figure out some sort of mystery? *The Case of Stone's Throw Island.* Ha."

"I don't know," Eli answered. He remembered how she'd embarrassed him that morning in the solarium. Was she acting this way again because she was too scared to consider the truth? "Maybe."

Josie sighed slowly, her breath fluttering nervously. "We're only here for a couple days. The wedding will happen. It will be exactly what Aimee and Bruno dreamed, and then we'll go home to our normal lives. Is yours really so boring that you need to look for adventure around every corner?"

"I wasn't looking for adventure. Adventure found me." Eli felt strange sitting on her bed while she stood beside it, glaring at him.

Josie blinked and then said, "Adventure is a choice."

"It may be a choice if you choose to live your life with your eyes closed, ignoring everything that's happening around you. Since when are you so gung ho on this whole wedding thing, anyway? I thought we were on the same page."

"So you're willing to sabotage your own sister's wedding?"

"Sabotage? Who said anything about sabotage?"

"What do you think will happen if we keep going on about this? Are you hoping the party will turn into one giant ghost hunt that you can turn into a graphic novel someday?"

"It's not like that. It's about finding out the truth. All I'm saying is that a stupid wedding shouldn't stop that from happening."

"And I'm saying that it should! This is not about you and me. This isn't about what we want. Right now, we are characters in someone else's story."

"Exactly! The story of the girl and the island and what happened here."

"No. The story belongs to Bruno and Aimee. They are the reason we're here."

"You sound like our parents."

Josie blushed. She lowered her voice. "What will it hurt to keep quiet about all this? To go downstairs and sit and listen to everyone moan about the weather? I brought a book to read. I've got games on my phone. Don't you?"

"Yes, but —"

"Good. Then let's get out of here. Let's stay with the others. And let's just be . . . ordinary for a while."

"You really think looking deeper into what's happening here will ruin the wedding?"

Josie laughed. "Well, it's not going to make it better."

Eli felt his face go slack with disappointment. "I know what you're doing."

Josie crossed her arms and knitted her dark eyebrows. "And what's that?"

"You're scared."

Josie scoffed. "If I'm scared, maybe it's because you're scaring me."

"I'm only stating what seems obvious!"

"Yes, but it's more complicated than *what's obvious*. Please. I don't want to be in here anymore. In case . . ." Josie cleared her throat and then made for the bedroom door.

"*In case?*" He knew exactly how she was going to finish the sentence, but he wanted to hear her say it.

*In case the girl comes back.*

"In case . . . anyone is wondering where we are."

# CHAPTER TWENTY-SIX

THEY SPLIT UP. Eli stomped off down the stairs and into a long hallway on the first floor of the house, while Josie found her mother sitting with Cynthia Barker in a small parlor just off the foyer. They were curling red ribbon with the edges of scissors, preparing decorations for the wedding.

Josie stood in the doorway, unnoticed by the two women, and listened briefly to their conversation. She was horrified to discover that they were talking about how they both felt too young to be grandparents — so horrified, in fact, that she didn't feel bad at all about interrupting them.

"Mom?"

Vivian and Cynthia both jumped, as if their chairs had given off a small electric pulse. "Hey there!" said Vivian. "Where've you been? What've you been up to?"

"Oh, you know. Exploring. We went fishing earlier. I caught a boot, and Eli almost fell off the dock." Funny, Josie thought, how those were the moments of the morning that she chose to share. Easy. Silly. What her family wanted to hear.

Vivian and Cynthia laughed politely.

"Mom, can I, uh, talk to you for a minute?"

Vivian scrunched up her forehead. "Of course, honey," she answered. Cynthia read the cue and excused herself. Josie took her place in the tall, straight-backed chair by the window. Outside, the rain and wind whistled and whined.

As her mother stared with concern, Josie thought about Eli and his stories. His theories. Upstairs, he had been right — she *was* scared. And now, although she'd be slightly ashamed to admit it, she found herself behaving in a way she'd thought she'd long outgrown: She'd come to her mother for comfort.

"What is it?" asked Vivian. "Aren't you having fun? Is Eli being nice?" She lowered her voice. "Cynthia says he can be a little . . . fiery."

"Eli's fine. *And* fiery. Whatever. I can be fiery too. This isn't about Eli. I just have a question for you."

Vivian waited, curious.

"Have you ever seen a ghost?" Josie asked.

Immediately, her mother's face grew grim. "Josephine," she said. "We did not come all this way for nonsense like this. The wedding is in a day and a half. Everyone is stressed out. Please don't be starting anything."

"I'm not! It's just —"

"Did Eli plant this idea in your head? His father says —"

"His father's a jerk," Josie snapped.

Vivian recoiled. "*His father* is about to become part of our family. I don't want to hear you say that again." She blinked and then added, "Even if it's slightly true."

Josie withheld a smile. "This isn't about Eli. Mom, I just really need to know." She reached out and placed her hand on her mother's knee. "*Have you ever seen a ghost?*" she asked again.

Vivian sighed, softening. "No, honey. I don't believe I have."

"But you think it's possible? To see ghosts, I mean."

"I don't know. Plenty of people seem to think so."

"Do you think they can hurt us?"

"No," said Vivian immediately. "No way."

"You're just saying that to shut me up."

"Excuse me, miss, I'm not saying it *only* to shut you up. I also think it's true."

"So, if there were ghosts on this island, they'd be harmless, right?"

"Josephine!"

"It's just a question!"

Vivian glanced over her shoulder toward the doorway, as if worried that another member of the wedding party might be listening in. "Why are you asking it? What happened?"

Josie's throat felt like sandpaper. "What would you say if I told you that I've seen a girl in my room?"

Vivian squinted. "What girl? Who?"

"Just a girl. I don't know who. She's come into my room twice. She doesn't speak, and then she disappears into my closet."

Vivian pursed her lips, as if suddenly coming to her senses. "I'd say we should ask the Gagnons who she is," she said.

"I already mentioned her to them. They were really weird about it. They insisted that there was no girl. Beatrice thought that I dreamed her."

"But you *saw* her?"

"Eli too."

Vivian hunched her spine and lowered her voice. "Did Eli see her first?"

"No! It wasn't like that."

"Did *he* tell you that the girl was a ghost?"

Josie closed her eyes. She should have known this would be a pointless exercise. She could go on sharing the rest of her experiences — the fort, the wailing, the wind — but her mother's disinterest was already apparent, written in furrows on her forehead.

"Listen, Josie, why don't you stay by me for the rest of the afternoon. You can help me prepare my little speech for the ceremony. It'll be a mom-and-daughter sort of deal. What do you say?"

Josie felt prickly at the words *mom* and *daughter* put together in that way — she and Vivian had never been a *mom* and *daughter* pair. But as Josie absorbed the idea, she found that it soothed her. "Okay," she answered. "But don't mention what I said to the Barkers. I'm not sure what I saw exactly, but I don't want to get Eli in trouble." She whispered, "His dad really is a jerk."

Vivian blinked and then nodded. "Deal."

# CHAPTER TWENTY-SEVEN

AT THE FAR END of a long series of rooms, Eli came through a doorway and found himself inside a large chamber, the walls of which were lined with bookshelves. Until he'd stumbled upon it, he hadn't realized he'd been wishing to find such a place. The answers to all his questions about Stone's Throw Island might be hidden in one of these volumes. Maybe there was an old journal or a photo album nestled secretly on the crowded shelves. Or better yet, what if Eli discovered a yellowed and brittle handwritten note tucked inside a dusty old novel?

He thought of what Josie'd said minutes earlier, while they were upstairs in her room. *Let's just be ordinary for a while.*

In other words, sit down, shut up, fold your hands, no elbows on the table, do as Mommy and Daddy insist. But he couldn't stop the image of the girl racing down the hallway from flickering through his memory. On top of everything else he'd already experienced that day. *Ordinary for a while?* Ordinary like when he and Aimee were younger and she'd treated him like a human being? Ordinary like before she went away and everything changed? *Ordinary for a while.* In a house like this, where secrets had collected in its nooks and corners like dust bunnies? He wasn't even sure what *ordinary* meant.

As he ran his finger along the edges of the nearest books, he noticed something odd about them. Each one appeared to be in pristine condition, as if no one had cracked any of them open. He glanced at the titles and the authors. All of them famous, all of them the big bestsellers he'd seen in the front window of the local bookseller on the main street of his town.

He stepped back, craning his neck as he peered up to the topmost shelves. Out of hundreds of books, there didn't appear to be a single one that could have been here for more than a year.

The corporation that had bought the property must have added a collection of books that they thought guests would want to read. Mysteries. Romances. Thrillers. Histories. New books were a nice sentiment, Eli thought, but he couldn't help feeling disappointed imagining what he might have once found here.

The wind threw itself against the windows of the library, rattling the glass harder now. The thick velvet curtains were open. They rippled lazily as air pushed itself through old seams between the wooden frames. Rain sprayed the side of the house in harsh spurts.

Eli plucked a thin hardcover from a nearby shelf and leafed through it. On the cover, a statue of a girl stared out at him, her arms extended, holding out a stone book as if in offering. The description on the jacket looked creepy and compelling — ghosts and monsters and kids trying to solve the mystery of an author who'd gone missing. An appropriate read for an unexpectedly rainy day.

Feeling suddenly exhausted, Eli plopped down into one of the soft chairs in the corner of the room and opened to the first page. But voices drifted through the doorway from down the corridor. They pulled his attention away from the book before he'd even read the first sentence.

# Chapter Twenty-Eight

"*ALLES LÄUFT NACH PLAN.*" This voice, whispered harshly, was now coming from the adjacent room, just through the doorway opposite Eli's chair.

"*Nein. Sie müssen diese Gehorsamsverweigerung stoppen. Agent Coombs weiß was er tut. Wir warten auf die Dunkelheit, wie er es befohlen hat.*"

Eli closed the book and hugged it to his chest. The second voice was familiar — deep, fuzzy — but the accent of the language muddled his mind and masked the speaker's identity. He tucked his legs up underneath him, as if he might disappear into the soft cushions of the seat. He'd been able to comprehend the words *Agent Coombs* — clearly a name — but the unfamiliar sound of the rest of the German buzzed Eli's brain, bringing him back to the cavern under the fort. The call for help echoed in his memory.

"*Aber unsere Belohnung ist in Reichweite. Warum verzögern wir das, um diese Spiele zu spielen?*" The first voice again, also familiar. High-pitched. Nasal.

"*Keine Fragen. Wegtreten. Dies ist Ihre letzte Warnung.*"

What were they saying? Eli held his breath, feeling it suddenly important that whoever was speaking not know that he was listening. He shifted in his chair, and a floorboard creaked beneath him.

The voices stopped, as if aware of his presence. As quick as lightning, Eli slipped from the chair toward the window, pulling the dark curtain in front of himself and leaning into the wall. He hugged the book to his chest. Then he turned toward a moth-eaten hole in the fabric through which he could make out vague impressions of his surroundings.

Two silhouettes filled the open doorway. One tall. One short.

"Is someone there?" asked the tall person, using the same deep, fuzzy voice that had been speaking German only seconds earlier. Now, with the cover of the foreign language removed, it was clear to Eli that the voice belonged to Bruno, Josie's brother. The realization hit him like a fist in his gut.

He braced himself as his mind rushed to fill in the gaps that his fear had eaten away. If Josie had studied German in school, it stood to reason that her brother had done the same. Okay then, thought Eli. But who was the man Bruno had been arguing with?

"Only the wind," said the shorter person. Eli recognized him immediately. It was Charlie Gagnon, the caretaker. "Trust me. I know this house like the back of my hand."

Eli held his hand to his mouth. Something was very wrong here. He could feel it the same way one experiences static electricity, like a subtle shift in the air.

"*Komm schon*," said Bruno, grasping Charlie's shoulder. "I want to settle everything with the others. Make sure we're all together in this."

As their footfalls echoed into the distance, dissipating into the depths of the house, Eli crept out from behind the curtain. He needed to tell Josie what he'd just witnessed.

# CHAPTER TWENTY-NINE

ELI RACED FROM the library through the sitting rooms that separated the eastern wing of the house from the foyer's grand staircase, skipping over dark wooden thresholds that met glossy white marble, avoiding the edges of wrinkled rugs and claw-footed furniture. By the time he'd reached the hallway that led to the rear of the house, the book he'd taken from the shelf had nearly slipped out from under his arm. He listened intently for the sound of Josie's voice and was surprised when, standing outside of the kitchen, he heard a joyful burst of laughter echo from the solarium. Turning to look, he saw Josie sitting with her mother at one of the small tables, shuffling a deck of cards.

Eli paused to catch his breath, his face burning red. Josie sounded like she was enjoying herself. And here he was freaking out. She hadn't been kidding when she'd said that she wanted to move on. What would she do when she saw him?

Turning into the kitchen doorway, he headed to the sink and splashed water onto his face. Through another door, steps away, he could hear Margo Lintel talking with her assistant, Gregory. They both sounded upset, saying something about contingency plans. Eli pulled himself away and went back toward the solarium, determined to reach Josie before he lost the nerve to share his new story.

At the small glass table in the solarium, Josie chuckled with her mother as they placed the playing cards onto the table between them. Vivian was the first to glance at him. A look of frustration flashed across her brow, but she smiled and said hello. Josie turned and forced a laugh when she saw him. "Hey, Eli," she said, raising her voice over the patter of the rain against the glass cage surrounding them. "My mom was teaching me how to play Old Maid. Appropriate for a wedding weekend, right, Mom?"

"Absolutely appropriate," Vivian answered, glancing down at her hand. "But don't mention it to Aimee."

Eli waited for an invitation, but neither of them extended one. "Cool," he said. "I was wandering around." He held up the book. "And I discovered a whole library at the other end of the house. Pretty interesting."

"Sweet," said Josie.

"And I know you mentioned that you wanted to do some reading today, so I thought, you know, I could show it to you. Maybe you could find something good too."

"Oh, well, I sort of promised my mom we'd play this game, so . . ."

Outside, the mass of tall pines swayed violently toward the house as wind gusted from beyond the cliffs. "Yeah, that's cool. I'll just wait here 'til you're done."

"We're going to be a while."

"Really?" Eli asked, the words slipping rudely from his lips.

"Maybe we'll join you after dinner, Eli," said Vivian, placing another pair of cards onto the table.

"But . . . I also sort of have something kind of important to tell you, Josie."

Eli watched as both Josie and her mother straightened their spines. Neither of them looked at him. "What is it?" Josie asked.

"I kind of thought I should —"

"I'd love to hear what you have to say," Vivian interrupted. The jovial atmosphere into which Eli had stumbled moments ago had evaporated, replaced by a cooler climate. Another gust of wind shook the solarium's windows. "No secrets in this family."

Eli felt like they were testing him. Maybe they already knew what he wanted to tell them. Maybe they were part of the German-language conspiracy. How would he know without asking them? "Okay, well . . . Do you know if Bruno can speak German?" Josie and Vivian turned at once to glance at him. Neither looked happy. "I only ask because Josie said she'd studied the language at school."

"For, like, two months, I did," Josie answered.

"I don't believe that Bruno ever learned German," Vivian added. "Do *you* speak German, Eli?" It sounded like she wanted to steer the conversation in a different direction.

"It's just, when I was over on the other side of the house, I heard Bruno talking with Charlie. But it sounded like they were speaking German."

Vivian chuckled. "You probably misheard them."

Eli soldiered on. "They mentioned the name *Agent Coombs*. Does that sound familiar?"

"Agent Coombs?" Vivian asked. "Who is Agent Coombs?"

"I have no idea. But it was all I could make out, because the rest of what they said was in —"

"German," Vivian concluded with a wry grin. Across the table, Josie sighed and stared into her lap.

"Yes . . . I mean, that's what it sounded like. It was really weird. Like, *spooky* weird. And I thought . . . well, since Josie and I already heard someone speaking what sounded like German earlier in the day —"

"Eli," Vivian interrupted again, "Josie's feeling a little exhausted from all this talk. That's why we came in here to play this game. Let's finish this conversation some other time. Okay, sweetie?"

"Mom!" Josie said, pushing her chair away from the table. "You don't have to be so rude."

"I wasn't being rude." Vivian gathered her cards together and glared at her daughter. "I was only trying to help."

"I'm sorry," said Eli, his face burning. "I shouldn't have mentioned it."

"No, no," said Vivian, standing, reaching out apologetically. "It's just been a long day. And this weather's getting scarier by the minute. I want to keep everything light. Fun. No offense, Eli."

"I just hoped Josie might have some ideas."

"Why not ask Bruno?" Josie blurted out. "He probably knows better than anyone whether he speaks German."

Eli felt his palms growing slick against the cover of the book he'd taken from the library. *Forget it*, he thought, turning toward the hallway. *I'll figure it out alone.*

# CHAPTER THIRTY

THE WIND CONTINUED to howl. Eli listened to it from the comfort of the big bed in his room upstairs. The clouds had grown so thick outside that the afternoon had given way to the darkness of evening a few hours earlier than anyone had expected. He passed the time reading his book by the light of the lamp on the bedside table, falling easily into the creepy adventure.

As the house creaked and the rain raged, his mind strayed every now and again from the story of the missing author to play with his memories of the day: the strange noises by the fort, the swastika button, the girl who kept disappearing into Josie's closet. And for this reason, a nugget of dread had fixed itself in Eli's chest, a sensation that he could not swallow down, no matter how hard he tried.

He was annoyed with Josie and Vivian. Josie had obviously shared with her mother some of what had happened, and her mother had tried to quell his curiosity. Eli hated whenever Aimee made him feel like an annoying little brother, but the feeling was magnified now that new members of his family were doing the same thing. They didn't even *know* him yet, so why would they judge him like this? This place was haunted. Or something. It was as if the island were alive, as if it were trying to tell them something. *No secrets in this family.* Josie could deny it all she wanted, but that wouldn't change the fact of what they'd both seen and heard.

Eli's stomach rumbled, and he looked at the antique clock next to the golden lamp. An appetizing aroma wafted into his room from the hallway, and he anticipated his mother calling for him several seconds before it happened. "Dinner!" Cynthia cried out from somewhere down the hall. Still Eli hesitated getting up and going downstairs. He wasn't sure if he was ready to look Josie in the eyes again. He also wasn't sure what he would say to Bruno. What if Vivian had told him what Eli had said? What if everyone laughed? Or worse, what if *no one* laughed? Would he survive the wedding feeling like a pariah — the idiot little brother of the blushing bride?

A creak sounded in the hall. Eli froze, listening. A moment later, a broad-shouldered but lanky silhouette appeared in the doorway. Josie reached up and grasped the frame. "You coming?" she asked.

Eli sighed uneasily, his breath whistling past his lips. "Right behind you."

As they walked down the hall, Josie glanced over her shoulder. "You really heard Bruno speaking German?"

"Yeah. I did. But I thought you didn't want to talk about it."

"What do you think it means?" she went on.

*Oh, so she is curious,* thought Eli. He paused at the top of the landing in the grand foyer. "You really want to know what I think?" he asked. Josie nodded, wide-eyed, serious. "You're not going to tell your mother on me?" This time, she shook her head. "I think that something on this island is playing with us. Something bad. Between everything that happened at the fort, and then hearing that totally bonkers conversation between Bruno and Charlie . . . it makes me wonder."

"Wonder about what?"

"We already talked about ghosts," Eli said. Josie rolled her eyes. "Hear me out. Your brother and Charlie did not sound like themselves. When they were talking, it was like they were, I don't know, possessed or something."

"Hoo-boy," Josie whispered, clutching the banister at the top of the stairs.

"Don't be like that. You asked what I thought."

"And your answer now is *possession*? Like . . . demons inhabit-ing living bodies? Like in that crazy movie with the evil girl and the pea soup?"

"Not demons. I was thinking spirits."

"Spirits? Like: *you see dead people*?"

"When you say it like that, it sounds ridiculous," said Eli. "But how else do we explain —"

"With logic," Josie snapped. "And reason." She shook her head. "I was more likely to go along with 'crazy cannibalistic family.' But *this* . . ." She laughed. "This is just too weird. My brother is not possessed, Eli, and he's not a monster." She turned and continued down the stairs.

"I'm not saying he's a monster!"

"What *are* you saying?"

"You know what?" Eli called after her. "From now on, I'm keeping my opinion to myself!"

"Good idea!" she shouted up from the bottom step.

# CHAPTER THIRTY-ONE

FOR DINNER, Beatrice and Charlie had laid out another spread, this time with a luxurious-looking seafood bisque and handmade lobster salad served in toasted hot-dog buns.

The group sat around the table in the dining room, tending an awkward quiet. Television static continued to blare from the great room — Otis had insisted they keep it on in case service was restored. The question that had been hovering over everyone for the past few hours was growing heavier, soaking with the weight of the downpour outside. *Should we stay or should we evacuate? And if so, how?*

Margo and Gregory had had no success in making contact with the mainland. According to Charlie, the little dinghy tied to the wharf would hold no more than five, and even that would be pushing it. What was more unsettling was that the Gagnons seemed to have differing views on what to do. Eli had overheard them arguing. Beatrice wanted Charlie to take the boat to Haggspoint and find help. Charlie insisted that they'd weathered worse storms than this, that the front would blow through in a few hours.

The rest of the party picked at their meals. Aimee looked pale and defeated. Bruno sat beside her, one-handedly rubbing her shoulder. *If he's possessed by anything at the moment,* Eli thought, *it's by compassion for my sister.* Despite the anger of the storm and his overactive fears, or maybe because of them, Eli suddenly hoped that Sunday would arrive with blue skies and cheers all around.

As dinner wound down, Vivian chatted quietly with Otis and Cynthia, all of them wearing looks of worry as the lightning continued to flash outside. Josie slumped in the chair beside her mother, staring at her untouched plate as if it were covered with garbage. Eli wished she would look up at him from across the table and make eye contact so he could silently apologize.

# THE SURGE

# FROM THE DIARY OF
## DORY M. SAUVAGE

Saturday, September 5, 1942

Dear Diary,

The storm has grown stronger.

And I'm not sure I am as fond of Emil Coombs as I was only this morning. He's proven himself to be a real spoilsport.

After the group discovered the muddy stones I'd placed in their shoes during dinner, Emil raised his voice and said a few words Daddy would have called "uncouth." I listened from down the hall. When Frankie and the girls laughed, Emil accused my brother of trying to turn them all against him. To "thwart" him. Screaming like someone out of his mind, he claimed he'd make them pay. This last part made the others become quite serious. I found my own cheeks burning. I hadn't thought that anyone would have become so furious. Frankie explained that no one had dirtied his shoes on purpose. "If we were to have fun at your expense, old boy," my brother asked, "why would we have sullied our own as well?"

This seemed to calm Emil, but he still insisted on finding the guilty party. When Frankie suggested that the answer might be ghosts, everyone chuckled nervously.

I must admit, this exchange has me reconsidering my visit. It was supposed to have been all in fun. I've already set several other tricks into motion. At this late hour, I worry that if I were to rush about, cleaning up every last one of them, I'd forfeit my status as secret stowaway. What if Emil reacts hostilely to my appearance? I don't believe I'm prepared for such a scolding, especially from him.

I must be careful in this secluded corner of the library. I shall hide here until I'm certain I can sneak back upstairs to the privacy of my secret space.

Oh, Diary, what have I done? I've no idea how to fix—

A crash has come from down the hallway. Oh, my heart races. It sounded like a glass or plate, or maybe even a piece of furniture breaking apart.

Now voices are shouting. What is going on?

Should I call out to Frankie? Or should I remain hidden?

One thing is for certain. Writing must wait until I can sort out what kind of trouble has found us.

Confidentially yours,

Dory M. Sauvage

# CHAPTER THIRTY-TWO

SONNY THAYER FLICKED his windshield wipers to the highest speed. They did little to clear the deluge of water that attacked his decade-old Toyota Camry, blurring his visibility of the twisted little road that veined the jagged coast near Haggspoint Harbor.

He slammed his fist into the center of his steering wheel, sending out a weak honking noise that barely rose over the holler of the relentless wind.

"Whoa, Gramps," said Rick, who was belted tightly into the passenger seat. "Take it easy."

Sonny eased around a sharp turn. Beyond the edge of the road, the earth dropped away. Another wild flash of lightning revealed the high tide that churned not far below. "Sorry. I'm kicking myself for waiting so long to do this. The storm makes no sense."

"Let's calm down. We'll get to the marina. And like you said, maybe we'll have more luck with the ship's radio."

"It makes me nervous that I haven't been able to reach Margo all day. I was sure she'd try to call. Something's gone wrong."

"Obviously. But we'll figure it out."

"Stupid television. Stupid forecasters. For all their gadgets and gizmos, what good does it do them? Or us, for that matter?" Sonny slammed on the breaks, and the car fishtailed before squealing to a halt. He threw his hands into the air. "I can't see for sin! If I were out on the water, I'd know exactly what to do. But driving this dumb car . . . Which way am I going?"

"We're almost there. The next left will be Harbor Street. You know what to do after that."

"Yeah. Drive straight and hope the dinghy's still moored to the wharf." Sonny flicked the turn signal and slowly pressed his foot against the gas.

For most of the day, Sonny Thayer had kept quiet about the bad feeling in his gut. It wasn't merely the clouds that had come in early, or the winds, or the drizzle that had started up in the afternoon. He couldn't stop thinking about the people he'd brought out to the island at sunrise. The trip shouldn't have bothered him; it could not have been more routine. But his intestines had started squelching soon after they'd anchored the *Sea Witch* back in Haggspoint Harbor. Nerves. Something was happening with the wedding party, he was certain. Most ship captains, at least the ones who sailed this far north, will tell you that half of their job is trusting their instincts. For Sonny, his current distress went beyond the job. Today, it felt like those folks were calling to him.

By sundown, he'd phoned Rick and asked him to come along to the marina. He'd told his grandson that he'd need help further securing the *Sea Witch* against the storm and also that he hoped to finally contact the party out on Stone's Throw. What he'd kept secret was his desire to take the ship out into the gulf. Sonny knew Rick would object to the journey, and he had spent most of the car ride trying to figure out a way to persuade him. So far, Sonny hadn't come up with anything that sounded half convincing, even to himself. It was going to be a tremendous challenge just to pilot their small dinghy out to where the *Sea Witch* was anchored several dozen yards offshore.

Harbor Street sloped down straight ahead. The parking lot appeared on the left, but Sonny drove the Camry all the way to the edge of the dock. The dinghy was secured at the end of the farthest slip.

Sonny pulled the keys from the engine but left the car lights blaring so he could see through the wash of rain, which was now blowing almost completely sideways. He flipped the hood of his coat up over his balding head and glanced at Rick, who was dressed in a bright yellow poncho.

"You ready for this?" Sonny asked.

"Absolutely not."

Together, the men leaped from the vehicle and scrambled out into the night. They made it to the end of the slip before noticing the trouble. The dinghy was right where it was supposed to be, its rubber bumpers knocking furiously against the wharf. The surge was coming in from the ocean, and the water was already treacherously high, almost at the lip of the dock. Beyond, out in the harbor where the ferry should have been anchored securely, there was darkness. The Camry's brights revealed nothing but the white-capped current.

Speechless, Sonny clutched the top of his hood, his fingertips digging into his scalp. The storm had somehow stolen the ferry from the harbor and dragged it upstream or inland to who knew where. That feeling in his gut squelched harder, and Sonny had to fight to keep down the microwaved macaroni and cheese he'd swallowed for dinner.

The deck wobbled in the surf, and Sonny felt himself toppling. Rick took his shoulder and steadied him. "Come on, Gramps! It's dangerous out here. I know it's not what you wanna hear, but we'll have to worry about the ferry tomorrow!"

Sonny shook his head and called out over the wind, unsure if his grandson could even hear him. "Tomorrow'll be too late!"

# Chapter Thirty-Three

Josie was tired. She was tired of being scared of the storm, tired of Eli's weird stories and odd glances, but mostly she was just tired in the way you feel tired when the day has beaten you down and you can think of nothing but sleep. So after dinner, while the adults continued to while the night away, drinking and talking and pretending that everything was going to be all right, Josie had climbed the stairs, brushed her teeth, and then changed into her aqua-blue cotton pajamas.

Under the comfy down blanket, she stared at the ceiling, which was painted with an amber glow from the bedside lamp. She listened to the wind batter the window. Eventually, the rattling became routine, just more white noise. Finally, for the first time that day, she allowed herself to feel at ease. *Tomorrow, the storm will have cleared*, she thought. *Dad will have arrived with Ama. I'll have more people to talk to and less to worry about.* She hoped.

Josie closed her eyes and thought of her friend Lisa Kowalski back on Staten Island. She imagined the race they'd run when she made it home on Monday. Lisa was fast, but Josie was faster. She smiled, thinking about how often she allowed Lisa to beat her in their races around the block. Maybe one day, when she was feeling brave, she'd tell Lisa why she let her win all those times.

Footsteps creaked in the hallway. One of the other guests getting ready for bed. Josie wondered if Eli had come upstairs yet. He'd seemed pretty down after dinner. She tried to force away her bad feelings about him, but her brain pushed back. She knew he believed the story he'd told — the one about Bruno speaking

German with the caretaker. Somewhere in her own mind, she wondered about the conclusions Eli'd come to. Possession? If it didn't seem *slightly* plausible, she would have laughed. She would have laughed so hard, it would have hurt.

Josie reached out to turn off the light, but a creaking noise at her bedroom door stopped her. She froze for a moment, then turned her head. To her surprise, the doorknob wobbled and then spun. She was so certain that Eli had come to bother her again, she rolled her eyes and prepared to scold him for not knocking.

The girl in the peach-colored dress slipped through the entry as she'd done earlier that day.

Josie scrambled backward toward the headboard, pulling the blanket up to her chin. Once more, the girl held her wet and muddy body against the door. "Who *are* you?" Josie struggled to shout, but it came out in a whisper. "What do you want?" Again, the girl ignored her; like before, she turned around and pressed her palms to the door. Josie knew what was coming next. The girl would dash across the room and disappear into the closet.

She understood. What she was seeing was not real. There was no girl. Whatever was happening here was like a movie, a single scene caught on a loop.

Before her doubts stopped her, Josie flipped away the blanket and leaped from the bed. She dashed toward the closet door and grabbed the knob just as the girl turned toward her. Josie swung the door open. The girl ran at her, and Josie clenched every muscle, preparing to be accosted or to have the door yanked from her grip. But the girl stepped past her into the dark and empty space. A cool draft followed. Josie watched as the girl, swallowed by shadows, lowered her shoulder as if to slam into the rear of the closet. But instead of colliding with the wall, the girl slipped right through it.

Josie yelped, unable to move, unsure if she should trust what she'd seen. The girl had evaporated. Gone, like dust into a vacuum cleaner's nozzle. Josie held her hand to her mouth and waited, as if the girl might pop back out. After a few seconds, Josie reached into the opening and touched the spot where the girl had disappeared. The wood panel was cold, and Josie flinched. She reached out again and knocked. A hollow sound reverberated. She and Eli had examined the closet earlier in the day, but they hadn't gone far enough — it was obvious now that there was an empty area on the other side of the back wall.

Her phone sat charging on the table beside the bed. Josie crept across the room, retrieved it, and then cautiously approached the closet again. Flicking on the phone's flashlight, Josie illuminated the cramped space. The white walls, the shelf, the wooden clothes rack all appeared the same as they had earlier.

She stepped inside, leaning close to the corners at the back. She ran her fingers along the seams where the edges of the walls met. Something told her to push. Hard. When she did, the wood seemed to snap, and a vertical crack appeared at the right joint, running from the floor to the base of the shelf above her head. She pushed again and the crack widened. With a third thrust, the right side of the rear wall moved several inches away from her.

The wall was a door! Josie and Eli hadn't noticed earlier because someone had painted over its seams some time ago, nearly sealing it shut. She examined the left side and realized that the hinges must be there, hidden from view.

*I am dreaming*, thought Josie, even though she knew she was wide-awake. That tired feeling that had earlier threatened to drag her off to sleep was gone.

The light shone through the crack, revealing a small room of raw wood slats and crumbling plaster. Thick cobwebs draped from these inner walls like elegantly decomposing tapestries.

For a moment, she worried what she'd do if she found the girl just inside the secret space, waiting for her. But the girl hadn't really been a ghost — she seemed to be a sort of echo. If *places* could be possessed, then that echo might be a clue. A hint toward some secret truth locked away on this island. And a *clue* was nothing to be scared of, was it?

Despite a slight tremble in her stomach, Josie pushed again at the panel, making a space wide enough to slip through. She held up the flashlight. Beyond a swarm of dust motes, the light revealed two vertical beams with several horizontal wooden posts bolted to them. A ladder was built into the wall. Glancing up, Josie saw the rungs disappear into a darkness that her light could not reach through. Holding her breath, she grasped one of the rungs above her head and began to climb. She was so concerned with what she was doing, trying hard not to drop her phone, that she didn't notice her heel knock against the secret panel and swing it shut behind her.

# CHAPTER THIRTY-FOUR

MARGO LINTEL HAD left the group once they'd settled into the den for after-dinner drinks. She wished them all good night, saluted Gregory as he chatted with Aimee and Bruno, then peeked in on Charlie and Beatrice in their private nook off the kitchen.

"Any luck with the radio?" she asked. From his chair by the cupola window, Charlie shook his head apologetically. "Well, we'll see Sonny tomorrow, I suppose." Margo feared that this tidbit would be of no help to her mother, who was probably having a fit at the nursing home. This storm was a doozy for folks who *didn't* have a phobia of bad weather. As she made her way upstairs to the small room she'd reserved for herself at the very end of the hall, she said a prayer that her brother, Robert, had had the foresight to spend the evening with their mother.

In bed, in the dark, Margo's mind roiled with worry. Though she'd kept her eyes closed for what felt like at least an hour, she did not sleep. Every creak of the house, every wail of the wind, every footstep of a guest coming up the stairs was like the breath of a little beast that sat heavy on her chest, wide-eyed and salivating, waiting to feed on her fear the moment she lost consciousness.

This was not how the weekend was supposed to begin. All of the notebooks she'd brought, all the graphs and charts she'd built to help keep herself organized, were useless against the onslaught of anxiety.

Margo drifted for a moment before another whop of thunder rolled across the night. She sat up, gasping for air, feeling her face flush with embarrassment even though she knew she was alone. When she'd caught her breath, she lay down again, cursing her brain for refusing to allow her to slip into dreaming.

But then something beside the bed shifted slightly. For a moment, Margo wondered if she *was* dreaming, for surely the silhouette that was standing over her must have been a manifestation of her overactive mind.

A hand came down over her face. It covered her nose and her mouth with a sweat-slick grip and squeezed. Margo tried to scream, but the perpetrator's palm was so broad, the pressure on her skin so tight, that barely any sound escaped. Eyes wide with panic, Margo looked up at the figure and struggled to make out her assailant's identity, but the shadows were like layers of veils, blindfolding her.

She pushed at the figure's chest, but the attacker managed to slap her hands away before pressing against her face even harder. Instinctively, she swung out her arm and brushed against the ceramic lamp that sat on the bedside table. She clasped it and then whipped it upward, feeling it collide with something solid. The attacker's head.

The lamp shattered. The person groaned and fell away. Margo rolled out of bed opposite the figure, opened her mouth, and inhaled deeply. This time her scream seemed to shake the very molecules of the darkness, giving the noise of the storm some true competition.

Her bedroom door opened and closed quickly, and she understood that the intruder had slipped away. Half relieved and half disappointed that she hadn't managed to beat whoever it was into a bloody pulp, Margo stumbled across the room and flicked on the overhead light. She swung open the door and peered into the hall-way to see if she might catch a glimpse of movement, a clue to where the trespasser had run.

Already, a few sleepy faces stared back at her. The boy, Eli, was standing in the hall several rooms down, his expression both weary and aghast. Beyond him, the boy's parents, Otis and Cynthia, had just cracked open their own door. No one said a word. They looked unsure of what was going on.

So Margo attempted to clarify. "I need help. Please. Someone just tried to kill me!"

# Chapter Thirty-Five

Josie climbed over the lip of the ladder, shining her flashlight before her. A long passage stretched ahead, a brick wall to her right and the house's roof sloping down on her left. Kneeling in this new dusty space, she felt her chest tighten. The rain pounding against the house created a din that seemed to drown out her thoughts.

Her skull began to throb. What exactly did she think she was doing? Shouldn't she at least climb back down and tell someone about what she'd found?

But a voice in her head (possibly not even her own) answered her. *The hour is late. What will anyone care? There's a storm raging and when it's over, they still have a wedding to prepare.*

She slowed her breathing and squinted into the darkness. She'd already made up her mind that the girl hadn't been real, that the island was somehow showing her a story like in a movie. If she eased back toward the ladder, would the movie stop playing? What if this was her only chance to find out what was going on in here? What if the answers she and Eli were looking for were right ahead, down this dark hallway?

"Hello?" she whispered. The echo of her voice led her forward. Crawling on her hands and knees, Josie tried to focus her light on the next few feet of wooden floor, but as she moved, her cell phone wavered, alternately illuminating the brick on one side and then the slanting roof on the other. After what felt like a long while, she reached the end of the brick wall, beyond which appeared a wide space with a low ceiling that stretched from the rear of the house all the way to the front.

From the safety of the tunnel, she examined this new room. In the opposite wall, a series of small rectangular windows near the floor reflected her light back at her. A bowlegged chair sat beside the nearest window, its blue velvet upholstery tattered at the seams and moth-eaten everywhere else. Directly across from it stood a compact wooden bookcase, upon one shelf of which lay a pile of thin hardcover books. Beside these sparse volumes were several delicate-looking china dolls, dressed in frilly and dust-encrusted dresses that looked like miniature costumes from the old film *Gone with the Wind*. A black steamer trunk sat on the floor, between the bookcase and the chair, a large, circular brass clasp embedded into its lid.

Taking it all in, Josie exhaled slowly. This had obviously been a child's hideaway. Maybe it belonged to the girl who'd led her here. But the space looked like it had been untouched for decades.

Shoving that aside, Josie wondered what she was meant to do now. She stared at the black trunk for a moment and a sticky feeling settled on her skin before seeping slowly into her bloodstream. "No," she whispered, with a strong suspicion of what she'd find if she opened the lid. "No, no, no. I didn't want this." But what had she *thought* she'd discover up here? A new friend? A playmate?

A sour taste filled her mouth. Her feet felt cemented to the floor. She wished Lisa were here. They'd clasp each other's hands and walk fearlessly together into (or out of) this strange attic. Maybe it *would* be best to bring someone else along before she ventured farther into the room. Josie sighed, realizing that she'd have to make do with Eli. She couldn't imagine what he would do when he saw this place. Probably flip out. Shout something like *I knew it!* But what other choice did she have?

Josie was about to turn back toward the ladder, when lightning flashed and a figure appeared, kneeling before the trunk. The flare faded, but the figure lingered, bright like the blur of sunlight that burns your retina after you glance at the sky. It was the girl in the muddy peach-colored dress.

# CHAPTER THIRTY-SIX

A FEW MINUTES AFTER the wedding planner's outburst, Eli found himself standing in the doorway of her room, watching the commotion of two families trying to sort out what to do.

Margo sat on the bed, dressed in a green plaid flannel nightgown, sobbing into her hands. Gregory knelt at her side, trying to get her to repeat the story. Eli's mother sat beside Margo, rubbing her back, and his father was bent over on the far side of the bed, examining the shattered remains of the lamp. In the bathroom across the hall, Vivian ran a cool stream of water over a facecloth that she would bring to Margo in a moment. Beatrice had earlier run up from downstairs to see about the commotion and was just now returning with a pitcher of drinking water. At the opposite end of the hallway, Aimee finally emerged from her room with Bruno in tow.

*But where is Josie?* Eli wondered. Hadn't she heard the screaming?

"What happened?" Aimee asked, her voice shaking. "What's going on?"

Eli stepped aside, allowing Beatrice and the others to pass into Margo's quarters. "Someone tried to kill the wedding planner," Eli said flatly.

He felt a sense of both wonder and dread, as well as growing satisfaction that his fears about the house were being revealed for the others to see. Of course, he'd wished Margo no harm, and he prickled with guilt when he realized that his mouth had twisted into a smirk. He raised his hand as if to wipe it away.

Aimee's eyes grew in disbelief. "Mom?" she called out suddenly, as if Aimee were the one in need of assistance. Cynthia left Margo's side, slipped across the room, and gathered her daughter in her arms. "Who would do such a thing?" Aimee whimpered into Cynthia's shoulder.

As Gregory recounted Margo's tale for the new arrivals, Eli leaned into the hallway, still curious about Josie. Maybe she was a heavy sleeper. Maybe she was listening to music through her headphones. Or maybe she just didn't care.

He was about to head toward her bedroom to see if light was visible from underneath her door, when a separate thought occurred to him. Someone else from the house hadn't come to check on Margo.

He glanced back toward the hubbub and counted heads. His mom and dad. Gregory and Margo. Bruno and Aimee. Vivian Sandoval stepped past him holding the cold compress. He counted himself and the absent Josie. Beatrice Gagnon stood by the window, pouring water into paper cups. That left just one person.

"Where is Mr. Gagnon?" Eli asked. Everyone stopped what they were doing and glanced up at him. After a second, they all looked back at one another, as if to confirm that the caretaker was, in fact, not among them. In that moment, Eli realized that his simple question had become an accusation.

# Chapter Thirty-Seven

WHEN JOSIE GASPED, the girl gave no indication that she knew of or cared about Josie's presence. She simply reached forward and raised the brass clasp on the trunk's lid. Josie watched, her hand firmly pressed to her mouth, as the girl lifted the lid and reached inside. Then, the girl sat back on her heels, holding something in her lap. Josie couldn't see what it was. She leaned farther into the room, trying to catch a glimpse.

The girl stiffened and whipped her head over her shoulder. Her eyes were wide with worry. She stared at the tunnel entry where Josie crouched. Was the girl looking at Josie or was she imagining that someone else was coming through the pitch-blackness behind her? Josie flashed her light into the dark, toward the hidden ladder. Nothing was there but dust swirling in the stale air and the continuous sound of the rain against the roof. She held her breath, trembling. Turning back toward the room, Josie stared at the girl and then whispered, "Can you see me?"

The figure blinked away, disappearing with a soft rasp, which may have been a gust of wind rushing through the eaves of the roof, or it may have been Josie's own ragged breath.

*Wow*, Josie thought. *Just . . . Wow.*

Though it had lasted only a moment, the vision of the girl opening the trunk filled her with a new courage. It had been like an instruction. *Yes. Do this.* She crawled into the room and stood, watching out for the wooden rafters that were inches above her head as well as the cobwebs that hung like delicate snares all around her. The floor creaked with every step. Josie moved purposefully, worried that the girl might appear with the next lightning burst. Once she reached the black trunk, she knelt. She wasn't sure what she'd find inside the box, but she knew that she'd never survive opening it without the comfort of the flashlight. She balanced her phone on top of her collarbone and then leaned her head to the left to grip it with the edge of her jaw. This kept the light steady.

The clasp opened easily. Josie grasped the top of the trunk. She lifted the lid, pushing it upward until it reached the point where it remained open on its own. She was still for several seconds, almost expecting something to jump out at her from the musty-smelling space.

The inside of the box appeared to be empty — a simple construction of dark wood. Josie grabbed the phone away from her clavicle and then shone the light directly at the crate's bottom. *What the heck?* Of every possible option, somehow she hadn't considered that the steamer trunk would simply be empty. She sighed and sat back, disappointed.

After a moment, she reached up to shut the lid, and as she did, she glanced once more into the trunk. Without the bold light shining directly onto the bottom, Josie noticed that the dark wood was not completely level. In fact, lying directly in the center was a small squarish object.

A book! Since its cover was the same dark brown as the wood beneath, it had been almost completely camouflaged. Josie quickly reached inside and pulled it out. Its cover was made of cracked leather, and the edges of the pages were slightly wrinkled, as if having survived decades of dampness.

Seconds later, Josie discovered herself sitting in the bowlegged chair across from the bookcase. The lid of the trunk was closed, but she didn't remember touching it again. That wasn't important, she knew. The book she'd found was on her lap, the cover open, black pen marks staring up from the front page. She'd read the words there several times, wishing again that she wasn't alone up here.

*The Diary of Dory M. Sauvage*

Dory Sauvage. Dory. Was that the girl's name?

Why hadn't Eli been the one to discover this place? Was it simply Josie's luck to have been assigned the room with the secret passage in the closet? She felt her cheeks burn. She'd cut off Eli, kept him from joining her in this quest, because she'd been scared. She knew she needed to find him immediately and show him her treasure. It belonged partially to him. At this point, who cared what his response would be?

But first, she'd peek inside, just to see what the book was all about.

She flipped through several pages, reading dates from the early 1940s.

She perused several passages: "*I cannot believe they didn't invite me!*" "*I haven't told anyone other than my roommate . . .*" "*. . . any light in the darkness can be revealing.*"

Interesting. According to the writings, once upon a time, this girl, Dory Sauvage, had lived on this island with her family. Apparently, Dory had been a little bit older than Josie. She wondered, would they have been friends if their lives had overlapped? If Dory *was* a ghost, could they be friends now?

As Josie sat idly in the chair — Dory's chair — an idea struck her so intensely that chills raced across her skin. If Dory's tale was important, the final passage should be the key as to why. Maybe Dory had written down what was on her mind on the night she'd placed the journal into the black trunk for the last time.

There was only one way to find out. Josie flipped to the back of the book and found the spot where the final entry began. She shone her flashlight at the page and read the date. *Sunday, September 6, 1942.* The first sentence was big and bold, written with a heavy hand that pressed the ink deeply into the paper.

IF YOU'RE READING THIS, I'M PROBABLY DEAD.

# CHAPTER THIRTY-EIGHT

IN THE BEDROOM at the end of the hall, the guests continued tending to Margo. Eli's question about Charlie's absence still hung unanswered among them. Standing in the doorway, Eli glanced at their faces, trying to read the secrets hidden inside.

Just then, the house shook, and from downstairs there came a massive crashing sound. Glass splintering. Bricks tumbling. The ruckus was so thunderous, it seemed as though the earth itself might have suddenly split in two. The lights flickered and then went out.

From close by, several screams erupted. Eli lost his bearings and stumbled against the doorframe. He heard a great whooshing resonance from below, as wind and rain whipped through the labyrinth of the house's hallways, ecstatic at long last to have gained entry to the grand mansion on the hill.

# Chapter Thirty-Nine

In the attic, another lightning flash filled the space, this one so bright that the world seemed to explode. A great booming sound erupted from somewhere nearby. Dust was shaken from the ceiling and rained down all around the room. Surprised, Josie slammed the cover of the journal shut and nearly threw it across the room.

*Stupid storm! Leave us alone!*

After a few seconds, she listened as the rain continued to spatter against the roof. Something must have crashed outside. Had a tree fallen nearby? Or had it been merely thunder?

She listened for further commotion, but none came. The white noise of the rain drowned out everything else. Not a big deal, she thought. But the book in her hands *was* a big deal. She opened it again.

IF YOU'RE READING THIS, I'M PROBABLY DEAD.

There was more to this passage, much more, but Josie understood that it wouldn't make much sense without the knowledge of everything that had come before.

She checked the battery on her phone. It had already diminished by half, but maybe it would be enough to keep her illuminated. Josie flipped to the front of the journal, settled into the rotting chair, and began to read.

# CHAPTER FORTY

ELI FOUND HIMSELF slumped on the floor, lying on his side. He didn't know how he'd come to be on the ground. But as a couple of dark figures dashed from Margo's room and tripped over his leg, he figured that, in the commotion, he may have been pushed.

"What's going on?" Aimee cried out.

"Everyone stay put!" Bruno shouted.

"Everybody move!" Beatrice called.

Lightning flashed through the window at the end of the hall, and for a moment, Eli could see that some of the group was heading toward the stairwell. Someone grasped him under his arms and lifted him to his feet. Eli glanced over his shoulder and made out Gregory's face smiling down at him. "Let's all stick together," Gregory said, turning to help Margo step over the threshold. He waved them both forward.

At the bottom of the stairs, Eli felt a brisk, moist wind rushing toward him from the rear of the house. A roar echoed all around him. Barefoot and practically blind, he bounded quickly across the cold marble floor, wishing to stay close to the dark figures ahead who were moving into the current. Moments later, Eli heard voices in the solarium.

"Oh my goodness!"

"Stay back!"

"Stop pushing!"

That's when Eli saw it. One of the ancient pines that had stood for so long on the cliff across the yard had fallen onto the house, crushing the enormous glass cage that, until minutes ago, had been the gathering place where the group had spent a good portion of that day.

"No!" Aimee shouted out when she saw the disaster. "This cannot be happening! Not now. *Not now!*"

Eli was stunned. The sky beyond the new hole in the house continued to flash white and red and green, with thunder quickly following. Rain spilled inside. Prickly green branches wavered in the wind like the fur of a felled beast. The wide tree trunk lay across the yard, a massive half circle of roots and earth lifted up from the edge of the cliff. Anyone sitting here five minutes earlier would have been flattened.

A spot of light appeared from behind the group, shining onto the debris that lay before them, and a voice called out. "Come away from there." Eli turned to find Charlie Gagnon in the kitchen across the hall, standing behind the wooden island in the center of the room, waving a flashlight, gesturing everyone toward what he believed to be safety.

# CHAPTER FORTY-ONE

CHARLIE LED THE GROUP into the small sitting room that was part of his and Beatrice's cloistered apartment and then closed the door against the wind and rain that continued to invade the house.

Nothing anyone was saying made much sense. Words. Words. Fragments of sentences. Filled with worry. Eli was sure that they were all in shock. Brains weren't performing optimally — his own included. Seconds ticked away, like in a dream where events and places and faces shift quickly.

Margo seemed to have forgotten about the terror she'd experienced upstairs, because she was already poised over the two-way radio, searching again for a signal. Or maybe she was simply desperate to escape from this place, from the people in this room, and the radio was her best hope.

Charlie handed out several more flashlights that he'd had stored in his bedroom closet. Otis and Bruno and Gregory helped examine everyone else, looking for nicks, scratches, or bruises, but the group seemed to be okay. All except for one . . .

"Charlie," Eli called out from his corner of the room. "Your forehead is bleeding."

Charlie glanced into a small rectangular mirror that was hanging on the wall next to the radio. He raised one hand and examined himself. His face was lit from below, casting crinkled shadows onto his sagging skin. There was clearly a stream of red running from a gash just at the edge of his hairline. "Shoot," he said.

Beatrice came up behind him and gasped. "That looks serious."

"Just after we'd gotten into bed, I heard a strange noise. I came out here to check on it. I was standing in the doorway to the solarium when the tree fell. Some glass must have got me good."

"I'll find a bandage." Beatrice rushed into the bathroom. The sound of water running from a faucet echoed into the parlor.

As Gregory explained what had happened upstairs to Margo, Charlie continued to stare into the mirror, a quizzical expression on his face. He looked like he didn't recognize himself. He dabbed at his wound. His fingers turned a tacky red.

"Why don't you sit down?" Otis said, taking Charlie by the shoulder and leading him to the chair by the cupola window.

Eli's esophagus gurgled. Did no one else see what had happened here? Someone had attacked Margo while she was sleeping, and she'd fought back. A broken lamp lay on the floor upstairs. The one adult who hadn't rushed to her aid was the same person who happened to have a head wound.

What was even more frightening was the thought that Charlie might be telling the truth. If he really *had* been injured by the shattered glass, then someone else had tried to hurt Margo. But who? And why?

Eli leaned against the wall, glancing at the faces of strangers and family alike, feeling suddenly exhausted.

"Where the heck is my daughter?" Vivian said, finally noticing Josie's absence. She stiffened and spun, glancing around the room as if Josie had simply been hiding among them all along.

"Wasn't she upstairs?" Margo asked. "I thought she came to my room."

"No, she didn't," said Eli. "Josie wasn't there. And neither was Charlie. Remember?"

Though the room was dim, lit by hash marks of flashlight, Eli noticed Charlie glare at him. Beatrice crossed before her husband, kneeling beside his chair, and dabbed at the blood with a damp towel. Eli felt warmth at his side. Margo had moved away from the radio and stood next to him. Her eyes were swollen. The skin around her mouth was red and chafed. His face flushed as he realized that she was staring at him with a look that said she knew exactly what he was thinking. The fear etched into her furrowed brow told him that she agreed with him wholeheartedly.

Bruno whispered, "You don't think Josie was downstairs when . . ." But he didn't finish, as if the idea of it was too terrible to say out loud.

"Maybe she's still in her bedroom," Eli offered.

"You really think she could have slept through all of this nonsense?" Otis grumbled.

Vivian swung open the parlor door. Wind blasted her hair back from her forehead. She called out, her voice panicked and raw, "Josephine Silvia Sandoval! Where are you?"

Bruno released his grip on Aimee's waist and followed his mother to the doorway. "I'll go get her," he said.

"I'm coming with you," Vivian said as Eli stepped quickly after her.

Apparently, no one wanted to be left alone on the ground floor with a gaping hole in the house and the possibility of a midnight assailant on the prowl, so the whole group ventured out into the yowling hallway and back to the foyer, where their thin flashlight beams lit the way up the stairs.

# CHAPTER FORTY-TWO

ELI CHASED BRUNO up the hallway to Josie's bedroom. Without knocking, Bruno thrust the door open and shouted out her name. Eli followed him into the room, and together they discovered that Josie was not there. Seconds later, the others crowded through the doorway, and the room that had, in the morning, seemed so spacious suddenly shrunk.

Eli checked under the bed to make sure that she wasn't hiding from them, though he couldn't imagine why she'd do such a thing.

The room flickered with pinkish-white light, and almost immediately afterward, thunder clapped, as if right above the house. Standing by the window, Bruno cried out. "There! She's outside!" He slammed his hand hard against the glass, indicating the direction he'd seen her heading.

Otis bumped into Bruno's shoulder. "Yes! Out on the spit. Just past that strip of trees. I saw her too."

"Oh my goodness," Vivian said, clutching one of the bedposts, as if to keep herself from dropping to the floor.

"By the fort?" Eli asked, sliding over the mattress toward the window. He pushed between them, trying to catch a glimpse. But the night was dark, and Eli could see nothing farther than the rain that blew several inches from the house. "What would she be doing out there?"

"Maybe something in *here* scared her," said Charlie, leaning against the doorframe behind them. The left side of his forehead was now covered by a large white bandage.

"That makes no sense," Vivian said. "Josie would never just run away. Especially not on a night like this. She'd never leave all of us behind."

"I know what I saw, Mom!" Bruno insisted. "It was Josie. She was sprinting toward that ruined building."

Vivian straightened up. She ran her fingers through her hair. "I'm going after her."

"Me too," said Bruno.

Aimee pushed through the crowd to be by his side. "You're not going anywhere without me."

"And me," said Eli.

"I don't know about that, Eli," said Cynthia.

"The kids aren't heading out there without me either," said Otis.

"I don't need you to protect me, Daddy."

"Don't argue, honey." Otis glanced at Eli and winked. It was so unlike him that Eli grew even more anxious.

"But, Otis . . ." Cynthia glanced around the room, as if suddenly realizing that she sounded insensitive. She quickly added, "Fine, we'll all go together."

"Great," said Bruno, moving toward the door.

Margo spoke up. "I hope I don't seem uncaring, but I think I may need to head back to my room."

"That's a good idea," said Charlie. "You're injured. So am I. We'll keep each other company."

Margo flinched. "I — I don't . . ." she stammered. Eli understood why: The number one suspect of her attack was offering to stay with her.

Gregory sidled up behind her. "Maybe we should all go together," he whispered.

"Yes," said Margo stiffly. "I think actually that may be best."

Bruno paused in the hallway just outside the door. "My sister is out there all alone. We're wasting time!"

Beatrice held on to her husband's arm. "We can't let them go without us, Charlie. We know every inch of the island."

"Super," Charlie answered brightly, seemingly unfazed by Margo's rejection. "It'll be a party."

# CHAPTER FORTY-THREE

IF ANY OF THEM had explored the closet, he or she might have noticed the crack in the right seam of the rear wall. He or she may have pushed on the panel and discovered the ladder leading up into darkness. Then, he or she would certainly have crawled through the long tunnel and found the room where Josie sat in the chair by the low window. But Bruno's claim that he'd seen his sister running across the far side of the island had distracted everyone. And Otis's confirmation that Josie was indeed outside had only spurred them along.

In the attic, Josie turned the journal pages quickly, engrossed in Dory's tale. By the time the wedding party had assembled their shoes and jackets, hats, scarves, and umbrellas, and had gathered in the foyer to head out onto the spit, Josie had reached Dory's final entry. Her mouth was gritty, and her eyes were sore. Her phone's battery was at a dangerously low level. But she couldn't stop now. Her imagination was whirling furiously, desperate to uncover what was to happen next.

# THE FLOOD

# FROM THE DIARY OF
# DORY M. SAUVAGE

Sunday, September 6, 1942

IF YOU'RE READING THIS, I'M PROBABLY DEAD.

I am writing from the secret space above my bedroom. It is after midnight. I am safe for now, but that safety could evaporate like a dream at any moment.

I'm so confused. I don't know exactly what happened or in what order, but I shall do my best to convey the events of the past few hours. You see, the Germans have invaded.

I have tried my best to keep the enemy at arm's length. I expect that this will not last for long. When I finish writing this tale, I shall drop the journal into the bottom of the crate in my attic. If I survive this night, I shall return for the book. If I don't make it, you should now understand why you're holding my diary in your hands. The enemy will have taken me.

It happened like this:

Earlier, while I was hiding in the library, I heard a commotion down the hall. Upon inspection, I discovered Emil Coombs standing over my brother with a rifle. He used it to strike Frankie in the face. Both Betty and Esther were shrieking in horror. I managed to sneak into the room just across the hallway. It took all of my strength to hold my own screams inside.

After a few minutes, I crept to the kitchen, where I thought I could radio the mainland for help. But before I reached the device, there was a sudden flash of lightning, and I noticed shadows moving through the sheets of rain in the backyard. Several figures were approaching the house.

I opened a cabinet and slipped inside. Shame weighs heavy on my shoulders that I didn't try to do anything to warn my brother and the girls. I wonder if I could have prevented what happened next, or if I too would have also been caught in the trap.

Soon, there was a crash at the back door by the solarium. Through a crack in the cabinet door, I saw several men pass by. They were dressed in military uniforms. When I heard them clamor down the hallway, calling out in their gruff German language, I began to hyperventilate.

I don't know why at that point I was surprised to hear Emil Coombs answer them. It still took me several minutes to understand his role in all of this. The lantern in the window upstairs. His agitation about my tricks. He'd planned out this trip as cleanly as I had. It came to me: Emil was a real-life secret agent. A handsome spy with a French accent, like something out of the movies! And my brother had led him to our island—unwittingly, I must believe—so that the Germans might gain a foothold, as my father had warned us they'd certainly try.

How could we be so stupid?

Everything else that happened, happened so quickly, I barely had time to think, never mind note every detail.

From the cabinet, I watched the few soldiers round up Frankie, Betty, and Esther. They were all crying, as confused as I was. Emil was shouting orders in another language, but I was able to sort out his intentions by watching his actions.

The soldiers led the trio out into the backyard at gunpoint, and I immediately worried where they were taking them. All that was out in that direction were the cliffs and, beyond those, the old fort that Daddy always tells us to never play in.

When I was sure that I was alone in the house, I grabbed a flashlight from the cabinet and then followed them. Down the hill. Through the woods. Up the rocky slope. Through the rain. I slunk along by memory, keeping the light off so I wouldn't give away my presence.

I held back, hiding around the corner of the fort's doorway, and watched as the soldiers forced my brother and the girls down the stairs to the cavern below. Their protests echoed into the night, dampened slightly by the sound of rain pounding on the rocks and the wild surf at the bottom of the cliffs.

Soon, the men came back up into the fort. I heard Emil mention something about making contact with a ship or a boat. A U-boat maybe, like the ones they talk about in the newsreels? I inferred that the rest of the crew would soon disembark and take the island. The men rushed past my hiding place, back toward the house. I nearly collapsed from fear.

When they were out of sight, I crept into the ruin. Once I was at the bottom of the steps, I whispered for Frankie not to worry. You can probably imagine his surprise to see me standing on the other side of the gate. I think they were all in shock, otherwise, they might have been trying to escape. As I examined what was holding the door shut — a pair of ancient handcuffs I'd once seen inside the jail cells below — I told them what I'd overheard. They were only half listening to me, paying more attention to the water that was filling the cavern, as it sometimes did during serious storms. I removed a bobby pin from my hair and fiddled with the lock. Thank goodness it worked.

Esther and Betty hugged me when we reached the top of the stairs, but Frankie reminded us that if we wanted to get off the island alive, we needed to act quickly.

It was then that he came up with the plan.

We three girls waited out at the fort while Frankie ran back to the house. He took one of my father's rifles and then revealed himself to the men. They gave chase. Gunfire exploded the night. Thankfully, my brother managed to avoid getting hit.

Frankie and I both knew that there was a part of the fort against the farthest wall where, if you shouted, your voice sounded like it was coming from the caves below. While Frankie raced across the spit, Esther and Betty hid there. I stayed out of sight. Once the men had come through the ruined doorway, the two called out. Their voices echoed as if from the cavern. The soldiers descended the staircase, splashing into the rising water.

Frankie and I went after them. Before they knew what had happened, we'd locked them inside. Frankie held the rifle on them, and quickly, I wrapped a chain around the same cuffs they'd used, so they'd have a more difficult time opening them than I had if they tried. I prayed that they didn't have the key.

As the water continued to rise, Frankie continued to point the rifle at the gate. He told them to toss their guns away into the water, implying that he'd let them out then. But he didn't let them out. We four waited and watched as the men shouted for us to help them, cursing us as the water reached their shoulders, their necks, their chins. At the last moment, Emil looked right at me, his sapphire eyes pleading with me. To release him. He knew I'd had a bit of a crush on him during his visits to our house on the mainland, so he was probably just as surprised as I was when I turned away and walked up the steps.

I didn't look back. Minutes later, when their cries stopped, I threw up. Esther and Betty held my hair out of my face.

Frankie rushed us all back to the house. Once inside, he raced for the radio and contacted the authorities. I don't remember what he said to them, but I remember thinking that more Germans soldiers were probably listening in from wherever they were stationed, translating the message.

Now, all we can do is wait.

I imagine a vessel offshore, hidden somewhere a bit farther than the length of a stone's throw across the water. This is why we remain inside. Frankie says that if we were to attempt to pilot the Yankee Girl back to Haggspoint, we'd risk being taken by the enemy. I am uncertain that we shall be saved. As we wait for the navy to arrive, I worry that more shadows will appear in the woods, moving through the rain toward the house.

I just want this to be over. When I close my eyes, all I see is Emil pleading with me. In my mind, I can still hear the men screaming for mercy. We had no other choice. Or did we?

Josie turned the page, but the writing ended abruptly. No signature this time. No careful good-bye. She closed her mouth, which had been hanging agape, and then glanced around as if Dory might be watching from the shadows.

# Chapter Forty-Four

In the feral darkness, ten figures struggled to cross the wide yard behind the house, careful to avoid the fallen pine. Though the heaviest rain seemed to have passed, unrelenting wind gusts throttled the group.

Charlie and Bruno led the way, shining pinpoints of light at the slowly sloping ground. Otis and Gregory followed up the rear with their own flashlights, making sure that no one tripped or twisted an ankle. By the time they reached the woods that marked the beginning of the spit, the umbrellas that Beatrice had lent to the group had been stolen away by the storm — one from Cynthia, one from Margo, and one from Beatrice's own hands — and were most likely stuck up in one of the tall trees that shuddered and waved high over their heads.

Everyone called out Josie's name again and again.

Eli stepped into the footprints of the men who walked ahead of him, onto the path where the grass abruptly changed to pine needle–covered muck. Heavy drops of water fell from the branches overhead, splashing onto his already soaked scalp, dripping down his forehead to the tip of his nose. Something was not sitting right in Eli's mind — something beyond the obvious. Eli'd spent the evening trying to erase Bruno and Charlie's weird conversation from his memory, but watching them plow forward through the forest brought it all back into focus.

*Agent Coombs.*

The name had given him chills when he'd first heard them speak it that afternoon. Now, somehow it felt as though Bruno and

Charlie were literally leading them down a dangerous path. Part of his brain told him that this was nonsense. Another part reminded him how strange it was that Josie had run out into the night, into the storm.

What if Bruno had been lying?

Hadn't Eli's own father backed him up, claiming he'd also seen her?

Eli didn't know what to think anymore.

The men clutched the flashlights, shining them forward, illuminating the trail. "Step lively, kiddo," said Otis from several paces behind Eli. He was holding Margo's arm, helping her across the rough terrain of the woods. He winked at Eli again, as if trying to lighten the mood but only managing to give his son goose bumps. "We don't want to get separated out here."

Eli hadn't noticed that he'd begun to slow down. His thoughts were dragging through the mud. He realized that the group was now passing the moss-covered tree trunk where he and Josie had stopped to rest early that morning, on their return trip from the fort, when they'd raced away from the cavern and its blood-curdling cries. The moment felt like it had occurred forever ago, but the voice that had shouted *Hilfe* tickled the back of Eli's neck, as if it had been waiting all day for him to pass this way again.

Otis used the flashlight to poke him between his shoulder blades. Eli rolled his eyes. Then he began to gallop forward, trying to catch up with the rest of the group.

# CHAPTER FORTY-FIVE

JOSIE STRUGGLED DOWN the ladder, clutching Dory's journal in one hand and her phone in the other. At the bottom rung, she pulled open the secret panel and crept into the bedroom, anxious to head down the hall, knock on Eli's door, and show him what she'd found.

The light on the table beside the bed was off. Hadn't she left it on?

She edged farther into the room. When she stepped into a cold damp patch on the wooden floor, she gasped and leaped away. Her flashlight revealed wet footprints and pine needles and bits of dirt all over the place. To her right, a greasy smudge had been smeared onto one of the windowpanes. Looking closer, Josie realized that the mark was a large handprint.

People had been here while she'd been upstairs reading Dory's diary — many people, from the looks of it. Maybe the whole wedding party.

But why?

Josie glanced at the door to the hall. It was wide-open. She tried the light switch but nothing happened. The power was out.

Peering into the hallway, Josie observed more muddy footprints soaked into the rug, leading to almost all of the bedrooms. It appeared that several other doors had also been left open. Only then did she notice that a breeze was blowing at her from the direction of the grand foyer. Had someone left the front door ajar too?

She tucked Dory's book under her arm. Eli's room was only several steps away. "Hello?" she called out, her voice muffled by the breeze. Josie shook her head, trying to clear away thoughts that didn't make sense. "Is anyone awake?" At the entry to Eli's room, she stopped and shone her flashlight inside. The bedding was rumpled, but nothing else seemed out of place.

Josie turned around, screaming out this time, "Mom?! Bruno?!" Her cry was met with an eerie quiet. For a moment, she wondered again if she was dreaming. But dreaming had never felt this real. Or terrifying.

Dory's tale scratched at Josie's imagination like a fingernail trying to tear a hole in a piece of fabric. It was almost as if, when she'd climbed the ladder into the secret room, everything in the journal had somehow come true: The Nazis had invaded again.

On a basic, rational level, Josie knew that things like this were out of the question, but the longer she listened to the wind shrieking through the hallways of the house, the more likely it seemed that the membrane that separated the impossible from the possible had grown dangerously thin. What had the chances been that, more than seventy years ago, Dory's family would be held hostage by the crew of a Nazi submarine? Not large. But Josie was beginning to understand that so much of life seems impossible only until that impossible thing actually happens. Love. War. Family.

Screaming resounded from the foyer — a crowd of voices, male and female, crying out in what sounded like fear and disbelief. Maybe there were words being spoken, but to Josie, it was one big horrifying jumble of noise. Barefoot and feeling totally unprepared, she raised her flashlight like a weapon against the dark.

# CHAPTER FORTY-SIX

WHEN JOSIE MADE it to the bottom of the stairs, the screaming had stopped. Now, a screech of wind echoed from the rear of the house. The night's voice was disorienting.

She followed the glow of her flashlight into the dark hallway underneath the foyer balcony. Part of her expected to find the wedding party sitting in one of the many rooms that branched off to her left and right, chatting and drinking and arguing as they'd done earlier that day. Another part of her imagined finding their pale, cold bodies piled in a corner somewhere. "M-Mom?" Josie called out again, weakly this time.

A shadowy figure crossed her path, moving from one doorway to another on the opposite side of the hall. A few seconds later, when she'd managed to unfreeze her joints, Josie leaned across the threshold where the figure had disappeared.

The room was small. The walls were a dark wood. A couple of chairs sat in the far corner, in front of a tall window. A flicker of lightning from outside revealed the outline of someone crouched behind one of the chairs. A pale peach dress. Dark bobbed hair. Josie only caught a glimpse of her, but she was certain she knew who she was. "Dory?" she whispered.

"*Stop!*" a voice echoed out from across the hall.

Josie spun as another lightning flash filled the house. In the brief burst of light, she saw a skinny young man she did not recognize raise a long thin object over his head and swing it down sharply toward another man kneeling before him. She recognized the object as a rifle as its butt careened into the kneeling man's forehead.

"No!" Josie instinctually cried out, immediately regretting making a sound. A moment later, when she shone her flashlight into this new room, she found that it was empty. Josie glanced over her shoulder into the wood-paneled room and realized that Dory had disappeared.

Were these visions the island's wicked memories? If so, the man with the rifle must have been Emil Coombs, the Nazi spy, and his poor victim, who'd been kneeling before him, was Frankie Sauvage, Dory's brother. She'd read about that moment in Dory's journal. Josie's own head ached as she imagined what that blow must have felt like. There was something safe in thinking that these images were simply like a film. But what if they weren't? What if there were real spirits here? Spirits who were seeking blood?

Horrible thoughts raced through her mind, and Josie grew even more worried about locating the missing wedding party. A gust of wind spat droplets of water at her from down the hallway. Josie continued onward. "Mom! Bruno!" She fought to keep her chin from wobbling as she added, "Eli? Where the heck are you?"

# CHAPTER FORTY-SEVEN

EVERYONE PAUSED AT the end of the forest trail. Up the rocky slope, the ruined walls of the fort stood like a black curtain in front of a darkened stage. Bruno shouted over the wind, pointing, "I saw her go through the doorway. She's got to be in there somewhere."

"For heaven's sake," Vivian mumbled to herself, shaking her head in disbelief. "What is she thinking?"

Bruno waved for everyone to follow him, but Eli planted his feet.

"Wait!" Eli called out. A bad feeling was spiraling in the vortex of his mind. "You didn't say she went through the doorway." The group continued on as if they hadn't heard him, so he shouted louder, "Stop!"

"What are you talking about, Eli?" Aimee asked, flipping her wet hair away from her face. "We don't have time for this!"

"Back in the house, Bruno said that Josie was sprinting up the hill on the other side of the forest. He didn't say anything about her *going through the doorway*."

"Whatever!" said Bruno. "That's where she went."

"Hold on!" Vivian cried out. She clasped Eli's shoulder. "Eli's right. That's not what you said earlier. Are you sure?"

"Maybe I was being unclear before," said Bruno, "but it's what I meant to say. You saw her too, Otis. Am I wrong?"

"Nope," said Otis. "She was at the top of the hill, going into the ruined building."

"Dad!" Eli shouted. "It's not true! You said she was coming out of the forest. I remember!"

"What does it matter now?" said Charlie. He started toward the ruin, as if expecting everyone to follow him. "It's probably where she was headed anyway."

"Come on, Eli!" said Aimee. "Would you leave it alone? Let's just go find Josie so we can get back to the house."

Otis prodded Eli with the flashlight again, and the group began to move up toward the end of the spit.

# CHAPTER FORTY-EIGHT

A PINE TREE lay on its side in the solarium. Josie stood before it in awe. The sharp scent of its bleeding sap was overpowering.

The past hour wiggled in her brain like a worm, waking memories. While she'd been in the attic, hadn't there been a crashing boom? Yes, it had happened right before she'd started reading Dory's journal. It had shaken the floor. Dust had rained from the ceiling.

Maybe this was just another vision. She blinked and then reached out and plucked several sharp green needles from the tree. She pressed the tip of one into the palm of her hand. Pain stabbed at her skin.

When the astonishment of seeing the felled tree began to subside, Josie was flooded with a new kind of worry. Had anyone been sitting in the room when it had happened? Was this why no one was answering her? Dread numbed her extremities as she imagined bodies crushed underneath these heavy green branches. She stepped forward, careful not to cut her bare feet on the broken glass, and clambered up onto the closest and sturdiest branches. As she climbed over the rubble, she shoved the journal under one arm and waved the other to keep balance. When she was steady, she shone her phone's light downward, through the crisscrossing mesh of the broken tree, seeking out anything that looked like it may be a body part, a hand reaching out to her, a face silently imploring for help.

The farther she walked, the more certain she was that her fears were unfounded. All she noticed beneath her were remnants of the twisted cage that had once been the solarium, pieces of broken furniture, and endless glittering shards of glass. The pine had done severe damage, but apparently, only to the house itself.

Standing on a high branch close to the tree's trunk, Josie straightened up and glanced around. Above, the sky was like a black brew churning inside a witch's cauldron. Across the yard, the base of the pine had left a massive crater in the ground near the cliff. Its roots fanned outward, looking like skinny pieces of the funnel cakes her mother would buy for her at city street fairs.

Josie's eyes stung with frustration. She didn't know what to do.

As if in answer to an unspoken question, the clouds directly over the island flickered, and the yard lit up.

Shadows were moving at the tree line. Was it her family?

A few more seconds allowed her to see that the figures were men, dressed in colorless uniforms, clutching rifles. Dory's tale beat in Josie's head like a drum, and the details of *this vision* became clearer. These were crew members from the German submarine. But could they see her? She didn't wish to find out.

With her tongue swelling in her mouth, Josie tried to turn around quietly, but the branches shook and creaked and cracked. She ducked down low, pine needles whipping in the wind over her head, and then she paused for nearly a minute, listening for any sounds coming from the yard.

Josie carefully worked her way back to solid ground, leaping the last few feet from the tree into the hallway just outside of the kitchen. Peering around the corner, she checked the yard. Empty. Still, she figured that the safest place at the moment was probably in her own bedroom. She would move the dresser in front of the door. And if she needed to, she could climb back up the ladder in the closet, giving herself an advantage over anyone who dared to follow her.

Without looking back, Josie raced to the foyer and then scrambled up the stairs two at a time. Soon, the doorway appeared before her. After she slammed the door shut, she leaned her back against it. Placing the book and her phone on the floor, she turned and pressed her palms against the wood. A warmth came over her face as she realized that her actions were like an echo of the actions she'd seen Dory doing all day long.

She stepped away, observing her arms, which were out-stretched before her. Her trembling hands suddenly seemed to belong to someone else. Josie shook her head, trying to knock away the feeling that the story of Stone's Throw Island was her own. She bent down and picked up the book and the phone. "No," Josie whispered, as if Dory could hear her. "I am not you. This never happened to me."

She hadn't noticed that she'd backed all the way across the room until she felt the windowpane against her spine. Its coolness shocked her and she spun. Her phone slipped from her fingers. Its light whirled wildly, bouncing from the floor to the walls and the ceiling. She bent down and picked it up, realizing that anyone who might be outside would now know exactly where she was. She turned off the light, and then, kneeling, she peered over the windowsill.

# Chapter Forty-Nine

"It matters," said Eli, walking beside Margo and Vivian. It felt like they were the only ones willing to listen to him at this point. "It matters because we came out here based on what they said. And now . . . Now it just seems like they're lying."

Aimee spun on him, fury igniting her eyes. "Stop it! Stop being a brat!" Eli felt himself flinch. "This isn't about you," she went on. "This whole weekend —" But then her gaze left his face and flicked up over his head. She stood straight, her expression going slack as she stared at the horizon.

Confused, Eli turned around and noticed what had caught her attention. On top of the hill, in the hulking mass of shadow that was the house, a soft light fluttered from inside one of the upstairs windows.

"Would you look at that," said Cynthia, her voice wobbling in awe. "Someone's back at the house."

The light winked out.

"Could it be Josie?" Margo asked.

"Either that," said Charlie, "or it's the person who attacked you, Margo. Searching for another victim."

Margo glared at him, clenching her hands into fists.

"That's Josie's flashlight," said Eli. "Violet, like the one on her phone."

"Eli's right," said Vivian. She faced Bruno, lowering her voice so that it was barely audible over the noise of the storm. "What aren't you telling us, Bruno?"

No one spoke for several seconds. Eli watched as the men traded strange looks. Bruno to Otis. Otis to Charlie. Charlie to Gregory. The four of them each stepped away from the group, shining their flashlights at the stony ground. Flecks of mica reflected back up into the misty air. Eli flinched when he noticed that the men were now standing in a diamond formation, surrounding the inner circle that included Aimee, Vivian, Cynthia, Margo, Beatrice, and himself. That bad feeling he'd experienced a few minutes earlier was transforming into something else — something resembling a hurricane.

"Bruno?" Vivian tried again, her voice a cricket chirp in the wind.

Bruno stared at his mother and his face changed. In the dim glow from the flashlights, his eyes squinted and became cold; his mouth drew down tightly, unnaturally. He almost looked as though someone had slipped a Bruno-shaped rubber mask onto a soulless department-store mannequin. Then, with a harsh voice totally unlike his own, he screamed at Vivian, *"Halts Maul!"*

The group in the center of the diamond drew closer together, too spooked to speak.

A moment later, Gregory looked across the diamond to Bruno and smiled. *"Sie verstehen nicht,"* he said.

*"Verzeihen Sie mir, Herr Coombs,"* Bruno answered, hanging his head.

*Coombs.* Eli remembered the name and his stomach dropped. Had Bruno just called Gregory Elliott, Margo's kindly assistant, *Coombs?*

*Agent Coombs?*

Eli glanced from his father to Charlie Gagnon. They were wearing similar smiles — thin and wide. A knifepoint ran up Eli's spine at the sight, goose bumps spreading across his skin.

Gregory focused on the group that was now huddled before him. "Forgive us, Madame Sandoval," he added. "They forget that their language is not your own. What 'Bruno' meant to say was: *Shut your mouth.*"

# CHAPTER FIFTY

THE MEN TIGHTENED around the rest of the search party like a noose around a neck. Eli took his mother's trembling arm and looked up into his father's flat gaze.

Gregory Elliott nodded up the hill toward the ruined fort. "*Schnell. Wir verschwenden Zeit.*"

Aimee released a loud barking laugh. "This is a joke, right?" Wearing a goofy, tired grin, she glanced at each of the men. "Prank the bride? Good one, guys. But really, you've taken this too —"

Before anyone realized what was happening, Bruno swung his hand up. A harsh smack resounded, and Aimee spun, falling into Vivian's arms. Vivian nearly buckled under the sudden weight of Aimee's body, but she steadied her feet and managed to hold the girl aloft. Cynthia, Beatrice, and Margo yelped in surprise.

Instinctively, Eli dashed toward Bruno, balling up his fists, aiming for the spot right below his belt buckle, but his father caught him by the shoulders. Eli rocked back and forth, trying to get away. Otis placed his thick forearm at the front of his neck, catching him under the chin. Just a little pressure against his throat was enough to make Eli's skull feel like it was about to pop. His body went limp, and he struggled to stay conscious, slowing his breath, focusing on the dim ruins at the top of the slope.

The women were too much in shock to say anything. Aimee sobbed, and the others clung to one another, as if that would be enough to stop what was happening here.

"No," said Gregory, continuing to smile. "This is not a joke. This is what we call *Rache. Revanche.* Revenge."

"*Revenge?*" Margo echoed. "Don't be ridiculous, Gregory! What could any of us possibly have done to you?" She touched her bruised mouth.

Gregory tilted his head in amusement. "I'm glad that you ask this. And you shall have your answer, Madame Lintel, in good time. In the interim, please call me Coombs. Emil Coombs. Your assistant has left you for now."

"What are you saying, *Gregory?*" Margo asked, placing special emphasis on his name. "You're talking crazy."

"My name is *Coombs!*" Gregory sniffed at her, displeased. "Stubborn," he added. "Just like your mother."

"My mother? You've . . . you've never met my mother."

"Haven't I?"

Margo's brow darkened. "You're the one who came into my room. You're the one who tried to . . . to hurt me."

"No," said Charlie from the other side of the diamond, waving his free hand. "That was me. Guilty."

Beatrice winced, as if her husband's sudden confession had stung her.

"Our arrangement was muddied briefly," said Gregory, glaring at Charlie with reproach, "but now we are all on the same page again. It will be better this way, Helmut, I promise. Much more meaningful."

Eli listened to the conversation through the sound of blood throbbing in his ears, his father's arm pressing at his Adam's apple. Did Gregory just call Charlie *Helmut?* The atmosphere around him shimmered, as if reality were beginning to collapse, and he understood that he was growing weaker.

"*Lasst uns gehen,*" said Gregory, waving his flashlight up the hill. "*Jetzt.*" Bruno, Charlie, and Gregory held out their arms, corralling Vivian, Cynthia, Margo, Beatrice, and Aimee like animals, directing them toward the ruined fort. Otis released his grip on

Eli's throat, and the world came rushing back. He gulped air, filling his lungs. His vision went black in patches. For a moment, Eli considered elbowing his father in the stomach and dashing away. Then he remembered the ferocity with which Bruno had struck his sister, and he understood that none of the men would hesitate to do the same thing to him, or to any of the others. He allowed his father to steer him as they walked. The ruin at the cliff seemed to grow as the group slowly made its way toward it.

In the moment before Bruno stepped through the doorway at the front of the crowd, Eli craned his neck back toward the house on the hill and shouted as loud as his lungs would let him. "Josie! Hide! HIDE!"

# CHAPTER FIFTY-ONE

A GLIMMER IN the distance beyond the woods caught Josie's eye. She stood and raised the sash. Leaning out into the spitting rain, she realized that there was a group of people out by the ruined fort.

Several beams of light revealed details that she immediately recognized: her mother's silver hair, Bruno's tall silhouette. All the other members of the party were out there too. But why? Why had they left her here alone in the house?

*Think!*

Impossibly, a voice rose over the sound of the wind and surf crashing against the rocky shore.

Briefly, Josie thought she heard someone call her name. Surprised, she knocked her head against the base of the window. The world seemed to spin, and the night filled with little glints of light. Another vision? Another illusion? The voice continued to shout, but then stopped abruptly.

Was that Eli? Josie rubbed at her temples, struggling to distinguish the twinkling silver specks that were swirling around her head from the lights in the distance. It was clear that he'd called her name, but what had the last few words been? They'd sounded like, "*Hi! Hi!*" but Josie knew that couldn't be right.

She rushed to the other side of the bed where her duffel bag lay on the floor. She tossed her phone and Dory's journal onto the mattress and then yanked off her soaked pajamas and pulled on a pair of jeans and a T-shirt. She slipped her boots on and then grabbed her jacket up off the floor. "I'm coming," she said quietly, foolishly, as if someone out there, or in here, could hear her. She pulled her hair away from her face and then reached for the book, which she dropped into her jacket pocket, and then grabbed the phone.

When she pressed the power button, nothing happened. The battery had died. She glanced at the open window, imagining the party in the distance. "Okay then." The curtains whipped at her. "Let's do this in the dark."

# CHAPTER FIFTY-TWO

THE WOMEN WERE screaming, the men were shouting, their voices intermingling with the cacophony of waves and wind and the crackling sky, turning their words into a new language, which sounded like an ancient language — the very first language, thought Eli. The language of *fear*.

He stood with the group at the top of the familiar stairway, by the curved wall of the fort, staring into the darkness below. The bottom few stairs had been enveloped by black water that was pulsing up and down, forward and backward into the tunnel that led to the old fort's prison. Eli pictured the rest of the cave already flooded, seawater pushed upward through the thin chasm in the far wall where he'd dropped the swastika button early in the day.

The men were shoving, and the women were pushing back. Teary and in shock, Aimee clutched at her father's shirt, begging him to come to his senses, but he jostled her coldly away. Beatrice pleaded with Charlie to stop this nonsense, but Charlie wouldn't look at her. Margo and Vivian had already taken several steps down, as if to simply get away from the grasping, uncaring hands of their captors.

"Go now!" shouted Bruno.

"It's your choice, *meine Freunde*," Gregory added. "Move of your own free will, or we shall move you ourselves. And I promise you, the second option will not feel very nice."

"Come on," Eli said, holding his mother's hand and taking the slippery stairs slowly, purposefully. "Let's do what they want."

"But why are they doing this?" Cynthia asked, her fingers crushing his own. "What's down there?"

"It's just a little room. Josie and I were here earlier today." Cynthia didn't seem to hear him. Her breath buckled and hitched. Gregory, or *Coombs*, or whoever he was, had already explained why they were doing this. Revenge. For *what* was still unclear. But Eli wouldn't worry his mother by repeating this to her. As he stepped into the sloshing water at the bottom of the stairs, he promised himself that he'd do anything to protect her. "Don't worry," he said, trying to keep his teeth from chattering. "This must be a big misunderstanding."

"I'm sure you're right, honey," Cynthia said, in a robotic and motherly tone — the one she used whenever Otis raised his voice at them during dinners at home. Eli guessed that she didn't believe her words any more than he did his own. "They're probably stressed out about the wedding. And the storm."

Nonsense. They both knew it. In fact, this last part felt so far from the truth, Eli couldn't think of a response that wasn't totally ridiculous. He went for it anyway. "I know!" he whispered, giddily. "Isn't it just *crazy*?" Somehow this made him feel better, if only for a moment.

# CHAPTER FIFTY-THREE

ONCE THE MEN had corralled the captives through the cavern's entry and swung the gate shut, Charlie Gagnon removed a rusted pair of handcuffs from his jacket pocket. He closed one loop on a single bar of the door and then clicked the other shut upon the loose doorframe.

"*Sind das die selben Handschellen?*" Otis asked, pinching the handcuff links.

"*Ja. Ich glaube schon,*" Charlie answered, nodding.

Otis raised his voice, rattling the cuffs against the gate. "*Die haben doch nicht funktioniert.*"

Gregory responded calmly. "*Einer von euch wird Wache stehen. Kein Problem.*"

The group inside huddled tightly together, not comprehending the men's argument but understanding that they had more pressing matters. Standing in an unsteady pool by the entry, they were unsure where their rocky landing might drop off into an abyss.

Charlie and Bruno perched on the steps behind Otis and Gregory, who were calf-deep in the rising water. The men aimed their flashlights into the faces of their prisoners and chuckled, as if taking delight in blinding them.

Gregory came up close to the gate. His light glared into Margo's face, but she steadied her lip and raised her chin. "So brave," he said. "How admirable." He glanced at the others. "Strong family stock. I suppose you deserve to hear the rest of the story now, otherwise, you'll never know why we're doing this. And what fun would that be?"

"You're sick!" Aimee screamed. "You're all sick!"

"You cannot be sick when you are dead," said Gregory.

"Dead?" Margo's voice wobbled.

For a moment, the men stared silently at the prisoners. Eventually, Gregory added, "Drowned with my men in this very place, over seventy years ago."

"Gregory, you're not thinking straight."

"Coombs, please!" he said. "My name is Emil Coombs. And yes, *I am thinking straight*. Our souls have been trapped here. Trapped until you arrived on this island, Madame Lintel. Your presence woke us up, and we slipped inside the skins of these men. I must admit, it feels quite strange to have a body after so many decades left helpless, with only salt air for breath. But it's nice. It's warm in here." He smiled and rubbed at his arms.

"Bruno!" Aimee called out. "Make him stop talking!"

Bruno stared at her and then chortled. The sound of his laughter echoed into the cavern and continued to mock them as they all shrunk back in disbelief.

Eli found his mother's hand and squeezed it.

"Please!" Margo wailed, her face turning tomato red in the glare from the flashlights. "We won't listen to this."

"You have no choice but to listen," Gregory went on. "During my life, I was an agent for the Reich. The great army had long planned an invasion of this continent. Our orders were to start small, setting up a communications base on this remote island. From the U-boat that we'd anchored a kilometer offshore, the crew could row over by raft. Once settled here, more *Unterseeboote* would bring more soldiers. We would spread north, west, south. We would bring more weapons. Gain control over more land, over more people. Spread the message of the Führer's Final Solution.

"At that time, this island had belonged to a family called Sauvage," Gregory added, smirking at Margo. Her mouth dropped open, and she released a squeak. "Sound familiar?" He didn't wait for a response. "While working undercover for the Nazis, I'd befriended the young man who happened to be the heir to the family fortune. Francois — *Frankie* — Sauvage. He told me about the island, and I hatched the plan. Communicated it to the Reich. They were very enthusiastic. Frankie took some convincing, but eventually he agreed to bring our gal pals out here, just the four of us. But when we got here, the campaign went awry. Frankie's little monster of a sister had stowed away, tricked my men, locked us in this cage. A storm rose up and flooded the cavern. Despite our cries for mercy, the savage siblings allowed the seawater to fill our lungs."

*Hilfe!* Eli remembered. *Help!* The events of the day were beginning to make a kind of twisted sense. "You got what you deserved," Eli whispered through clenched teeth. Aimee shushed him.

"The girl's name was Dory." Gregory stared into Margo's eyes for several seconds. "Madame Lintel, would you like to explain what this name means to you?"

Margo was quiet for a moment, before glancing at the water that was now lapping at her legs. "Dory Sauvage. Dorothea Marie Sauvage. She grew up and married, becoming *Thea* Petit. My mother."

# CHAPTER FIFTY-FOUR

SEVERAL STRANGE SECONDS passed while the men simply stared at the group trapped behind the black bars. The men smiled with satisfaction, as if soaking up all of their captives' panic, their terror, their helplessness. Then, like a flock of birds, the men turned at once and ascended the stairs to the main level of the fort. Without the flashlights, the cavern faded to black.

The women pleaded with them, called out their names, trying to penetrate the true selves of the men who must have been horrified to watch this atrocity from the prisons of their own minds.

Blind, Eli started to process what he'd just learned. *Dorothea Marie Sauvage. She grew up and married, becoming Thea Petit, my mother.* Petit must have been Margo's maiden name. Her mother had come to this island during that long-ago war. An image of the girl he and Josie had seen earlier that day snapped into his head. Could it be . . . ?

The women grappled the gate and rattled its hinges, begging for release. It was too complicated, too weird for them to consider the conversation they'd just heard. Though no one could see it, the water continued to rise, now tickling their shins.

"You're wasting your energy!" Eli cried out.

"And what do you suggest we do instead?" Aimee's voice came from the darkness.

"Listen," he said, as calmly as he could.

"I'm listening," Aimee answered, "but you're not talking."

"I'm not talking, but *they* are."

Above, the men were speaking. Eli thought he could make out the exchange as it bounced down the tunnel toward him.

Otis: *"Wir müssen in Kontakt treten."*

Gregory: *"Sie sind sich bewusst. Bald werden sie auferstehen."*

They went on and on, their words incomprehensible. Finally, the talk was lost to the wind.

"I don't understand," Aimee said wearily. "Bruno hit me. He *hit* me."

"It wasn't *Bruno*, honey," Margo answered. "Those people up there are not the men you know."

"So you believe them?" Vivian asked. "You believe that they've all been *taken over*?"

"What's our other option?" Beatrice asked. "To not believe them? It would seem that would leave us in the same predicament, would it not?"

"No," said Vivian. "It would not. I'd rather keep my sanity, thank you very much."

"You keep your sanity then," Aimee argued. "I'd rather get out of here."

"Being rude to your future mother-in-law isn't going to help," Cynthia chimed in. That kept Aimee quiet for a moment.

"I know something that might help," Eli offered.

"A way out?" Vivian asked.

"A story." Eli waited for someone to tell him to shut his mouth — *there is no time for this!* — but no one did. "It started almost as soon as we stepped foot on this island."

"What started?" Aimee asked.

The water lapped at the bottom of their kneecaps.

Eli sighed. "I was seeing things. Hearing things. I shared it all with Josie. We thought it might be ghosts. It sounds stupid now, saying it out loud —"

"Eli," said Margo, finding his shoulder with her hand and squeezing, "just tell us what happened."

# CHAPTER FIFTY-FIVE

IF JOSIE HADN'T made the trek out to the fort earlier that day, she might have ended up falling onto the jagged rocks on either edge of the spit. With no flashlight, the forest was a labyrinth of dips and turns and dead ends. But trusting her instincts and her memory, Josie assuredly placed one foot in front of the next and eventually found her way.

She ran. She ran like she did when she raced Lisa back home, only now she wasn't pulling punches. This time, she was determined to win.

By the time she reached the other side of the forest, she realized that her phone running out of battery might have been for the best. Certainly, she would have been tempted to shine the light the entire way. Now, she was cloaked in darkness, which gave her confidence to continue. Thankfully, no shadows appeared at the edges of her vision, no men holding rifles, and the lightning flashes were coming fewer and farther between.

Josie dashed the last part of the way, the cool air rushing into her lungs, clearing away everything inside that felt toxic. She was almost at the fort's gaping entrance, when she saw lights and heard voices. She was about to call out to them, to ask if they needed help, when she realized that the voices were not speaking English.

"*Meine Geschichte war erfolgreich. Sie folgten uns wie Schafe.*" Was that Bruno? Josie released a long, frustrated breath. German. It was just as Eli had insisted that afternoon. "*Jetzt müssen wir nach dem Mädchen suchen.*"

What did Bruno mean? *They followed us*, he'd said —
sort of — and then finished with something about *looking out for
a girl*?

Josie flinched and then swiveled her body against the outer
wall, hiding herself from the view of the men. She understood. *She*
was the girl. Eli's comment about Bruno and Charlie being possessed flashed through her memory, but she shoved it away. She
needed to concentrate.

"*Sie haben recht.*" This sounded like Gregory Elliott, Margo's
assistant. "*Wir werden nicht zulassen, dass uns noch eine Göre davon
abhält, unsere Pflicht zu tun.*"

*You are correct*, Gregory had said. Josie tried to piece the rest of
his words together. Something about *stopping* . . . something?

Ugh, this was hopeless!

What the heck were they doing? Couldn't she just ask them? If
they wanted to find her, maybe she should just show herself.

Josie was seriously considering stepping into the doorway
when she heard a woman's scream come from inside the fort. With
chills enveloping her, she hugged her rib cage tightly, feeling the
edge of Dory's journal from its spot in her jacket pocket. "Quiet!"
Bruno called back. "Do not make me say it again!" Josie's chills
turned to needle pricks. "Agent Coombs," he went on, "we are
wasting time. *Sie kann sich überall versteckt haben.*"

Josie's eyes popped open wide. Agent Coombs?

"Fine," said Gregory. "You stay here. Guard these *Dummköpfe*,
at least until they stop shrieking. The rest of us will go back and
search the house."

Footsteps shuffled across the wet, rocky ground. Flashlights
lit the edges of the fort's crumbling doorway. Josie held her breath,
pressing herself even harder against the stone wall, wishing she
had the ability to melt into its surface the way the vision of Dory

had done in her bedroom closet. She smelled the pungent odor of sweat and salt as the men passed several feet from where she stood. They hastened from the fort's entry, rushing toward the woods at the bottom of the slope. Their silvery torches gleamed, illuminating the wind-whipped and broken tops of the pines.

# Chapter Fifty-Six

By the time Eli finished his story, the water had reached his waist and was rising steadily. Its pulsing energy kept trying to knock him off his feet. He clung to the gate for stability and waited for a response from the rest of the group. For several long seconds, the only sound that filled the dark space was the endless echo of the surf.

Finally, someone — it sounded like Beatrice — spoke up. "How strong are those bars? If we all pull or push at once, maybe —"

"Say we get the door open," Vivian interrupted. "What happens when we try to go up those stairs?"

"One of them must be guarding the exit," said Aimee.

"We can't just stand here!" Cynthia cried out. Someone pushed at Eli, grabbing for the rusted handcuffs. Whoever it was gave the door a good shove and the metal clanged, reverberating in all directions like thunder.

"Keep it down!" said someone else. "They'll hear you!"

"Good!" said Beatrice. "Then maybe we can still get them to come to their senses!"

Eli clicked his tongue against the roof of his mouth. Had they not heard his tale, or were they ignoring him on purpose? If Eli was correct, none of the men were themselves any longer.

The force of the churning water knocked Eli into several shivering bodies nearby.

"Oof!" This was Margo. She'd been the quietest since the men had left them alone. Eli couldn't imagine what was going through her mind. According to Gregory, this was happening because of something that her mother had done over seventy years ago. Eli had so many questions he wished to ask her, but he knew if they didn't escape soon, none of the answers would matter.

"I can't get enough force," said Beatrice, who was standing by the gate. "The water's like sludge. Too much resistance."

"What about the crevice Eli mentioned?" said Aimee.

So Aimee'd been listening after all.

"The one where he dropped the button? What about it, dear?" Cynthia asked.

Wow, his mother had heard him too!

"If that's where the water is getting in," Aimee went on, "maybe it's feasible for one of us to use the crevice to somehow get out."

"That sounds extremely dangerous," her mother replied.

"What other options do we have?"

"The crevice is really slim," Eli added. "And who knows where it leads?"

"It leads to the sea caves beneath the fort," said Beatrice. "And beyond that, to the open water."

"Is this a real possibility, Beatrice?" Cynthia asked. "For escape?"

"If you have a death wish."

The tide sloshed them all forward, against the iron bars. The water level was now above Eli's belly button.

Aimee went on. "But there's a chance? Crevice leads to cave. Cave leads to ocean?"

"Yes," Beatrice added. "And ocean leads to sharp, sharp rocks, upon which the waves will most likely toss whoever is stupid enough to try it. That is, if she hasn't already drowned."

Eli closed his eyes. The darkness was the same as when he had them open. In his mind, he could hear the screaming — *Hilfe!* —

from early that morning. Those sailors had died with an icy shard of fear in their hearts. Eli couldn't allow that to happen to his family.

He pushed himself away from the group, away from the platform and the door, dropping down into the water, his head bobbing above the surface of the black pool. If his sense of direction was even mildly intact, he knew that the crevice should be directly below him. He took a mammoth breath, filling his lungs. The last thing he heard before plunging was his mother's voice, calling out to him, "Elias! No!"

# CHAPTER FIFTY-SEVEN

JOSIE PEERED THROUGH the doorway. Inside the fort, Bruno stood at the top of the stairway, his spine stiff and his arms straight at his sides. He held the flashlight at his hip, shining it at the ground. His face was lit by the reflection bouncing up from below. His eyes were pits of shadow, his lips pressed together, making his expression unreadable. He seemed to be staring at nothing, concentrating on being still, the way a soldier might behave while on guard duty, which, Josie sensed, he was. She squinted, trying to recognize the brother she knew in the statue-like figure who merely resembled him, but this only made everything blurry.

Josie picked up a stone and tossed it toward him. It clattered against the rocks several feet away. He spun, robotic, aiming the light as if he were clutching a pistol. While he was distracted, Josie stepped forward. "Bruno," she said. "I'm here." He snapped his head toward her. The beam of light soon followed, and Josie had to raise her hand to keep from being blinded. She imagined him opening his mouth to call to the other men, so she spoke quickly, trying to hold his attention. "I know everyone else is looking for me. But I wanted to come to you first. I wanted you to have the honor of capturing me. Agent Coombs will be pleased." It felt like the end of a make-believe game she'd once forced him to play.

Bruno lowered the light slightly so she could see his face. He looked curious, interested in what she was saying. Muffled voices rose from the hole behind him. The rest of the party was down there; she had a feeling that it was not by choice. "But you have to promise to let everyone else go."

Bruno smiled. To Josie's surprise, he held his arms open as if inviting her to come closer. She froze in wonder, hoping that the gesture was genuine, that he'd been only pretending while the other men were around. She was his little sister. He would do anything to help her.

She approached him, stopping about a foot away, and then looked up at him. "Bruno?" With the light now directed away, his face was a shroud of darkness. Still, she thought she saw him nod. "I knew you were in there somewhere," she said, wrapping her arms around his torso, pressing her cheek into his sturdy chest. He hugged her back. She felt her tears leak onto his shirt, dampening her already wet skin. "What's going on?" she asked. Her voice sounded so small, like it had when she'd been a toddler and he a teenager who seemed to know so much more of the world than she did. "I'm so confused." She pulled away, trying to glance up, to see into his eyes.

But Bruno squeezed her tight. Tighter. So tight, she could no longer move. So tight, she could barely breathe. *"Achtung!"* he called out to the night. *"Achtung! Das Mädchen ist hier!"*

"No," Josie wheezed. "Bruno . . . stop." She swung her shoulders sharply backward, one, then the other. When she realized she was trapped in his grasp, she screamed. Voices rose once again from the bottom of the stairs. She imagined the cavern filling with water like Dory had described.

Craning her head back, she tried one last time to see Bruno's face. But the man staring down at her, his brows knitted in fury, was not her brother. She whipped her head forward as hard as she could, making contact with his sternum. A crack rang out. This was followed by a blast of pain between her eyes. She wasn't sure if she had broken something in him or herself.

Bruno loosened his grip for a moment, and, without thinking, Josie threw all of her weight at him. His ankle twisted as his heel slipped off the top stair, and he fell backward, taking Josie with him. They tumbled down the steps, splashing into the water that had spilled out from inside the cave.

After a moment, the world stopped spinning, and Josie realized that her brother was limp beneath her. The lower halves of their bodies were submerged. His head was lying on one of the stone steps, his eyes closed. His arms were raised over his head and in his right hand was the flashlight. Josie snatched it from him, then scrambled away, backing into the dark tunnel.

The water was at her chest, but she barely noticed. Voices echoed from behind her, imploring her for help, but she didn't answer. She kept the light on Bruno, worried that he would wake up but also worried that he might never wake up.

# CHAPTER FIFTY-EIGHT

ELI WAS FLOATING in space, in a black abyss with no borders.

He swam, directing himself downward. Pressure squeezed at his chest. The swelling of the surf rocked him, as if trying to lull him to sleep. He raised his hands and clawed at the water. His body rocketed forward. He repeated this action, bringing himself deeper and deeper into the cavern, until his fingertips brushed the slimy stone floor.

He'd made it down, but in order to stay there, he'd have to release some of his breath. It bubbled out of his nostrils and disappeared into the darkness over his head. The dampened sound of the surf under the water was dreamlike.

*Is this a dream?*

*Stay focused!* he silently screamed at himself. He frog-kicked his legs and stretched his hands out ahead of him, searching for the wall. Within seconds, he made contact.

Blind, he pulled himself toward the crevice in the far corner. A moment later, he was clutching its rough periphery. Waving his hand back and forth just inside the hole, he gauged its width. It was only a couple of feet across. He might be able to fit. But there was no way he could try without surfacing for one last breath.

Behind his eyelids, a horrible image filled his mind. A uniformed man had floated here seventy years ago, exploring this same spot, trying to find a way out. The button that Eli had plucked from the rock that morning was proof of this. But the man had not made it out. He and his companions had lost their lives doing exactly what Eli was doing. What had made Eli think he'd be any more capable?

He imagined a hand reaching out from the crevice — fingernails crusted with green gunk, blue papery skin decorated with a pox of long-dead barnacles — and then grabbing his arm, dragging him into the sea caves beneath the fort. He spun and tried to push off from the wall. But his sneaker caught on something. Or something had caught him! He released a muffled howl of terror. Unfortunately, he exhaled the rest of his breath at the same time.

# CHAPTER FIFTY-NINE

THE BARS OF THE CAGE glowed white when Josie's flashlight struck them. Inside the cave, the faces of the women stared back, unsure whether to shout in fear or joy. Her mother's eyes went wide; her lips trembled. The tide was nearly at their shoulders now. Soon, they'd be treading water as it brought them buoyantly toward the ceiling.

"It's me!" Josie cried. And a wail of relief ricocheted up the tunnel. "Don't worry. I'm going to get you out." With the flashlight raised over her head, she kicked against the surge and hopped toward the door. When she was inches away, a hand reached from inside and stroked her cheek. "Mommy, don't worry," Josie said, holding back tears. "Please don't cry." But the plea was pointless; everyone was already crying, their voices a mix of unintelligible emotion.

She tried to yank open the door. It gave a few inches and then held fast. Glancing at the top of the cage, Josie noticed the pair of rusted handcuffs latching the door to the frame. She remembered seeing the cuffs earlier that day, attached to the bars inside one of the pocket cells in the cavern. Maybe Charlie had come out here after she and Eli had told him what they'd seen. Maybe he'd set this place up for what he and the others had planned — the plan that was unfolding right at this moment.

She thought of her brother lying on the stairs behind her and was suddenly nauseated. The men had all eaten dinner with them, provided comforting words about the storm, had pretended that everything was going to be fine. She wanted desperately to believe that they hadn't changed before that.

"Stand back," said Josie. She swung the butt end of the flashlight back before thrashing it against the cuffs. *Crash*. Again. *Crash*. Again. *Crash*. Again. *Clink*. Wide-eyed, Josie turned the light around. The beam revealed that the chain linking the cuffs was now broken. She was too surprised to do anything else but stare in awe at her handiwork.

The door swung outward and Josie came back into her body. Her mother's arms found her, enclosing her, reminding her of the moment she'd had with Bruno at the top of the stairs. Josie had to force away the impulse to push Vivian back.

Margo and Beatrice slipped past them, moving toward the stairway that would bring them up to the fort. But Cynthia and Aimee remained in the cavern. They were shouting, their raw voices coming from a primal place in their lungs. "Eli! Elias!"

"What's going on?" Josie asked.

"Eli said he knew a way out," answered her mother. "Something about sea caves? Then he dove down. He hasn't come back up."

"How long ago?" Josie asked. Vivian stared at her blankly. "Mom, how long has he been under?"

"I don't know," Vivian muttered, her teeth chattering. Josie pushed past her and through the doorway. "Honey, what are you doing? No!"

Turning away from her mother, she shone the flashlight at Aimee and Cynthia. They barely blinked as they continued to call Eli's name. "Which way did he go?" Josie interrupted. Aimee stopped screaming for a second and pointed, and Josie took a breath.

# CHAPTER SIXTY

THE SALT WATER stung Eli's eyes. He'd opened them in a panic when he found that he was stuck. And he'd kept them open even though he could not see.

He kicked and flailed his arms, certain that his vision of the lifeless hand creeping out from the crevice had come true. His chest pounded with pain. All he could think of was opening his mouth to catch more air, but a voice at the bottom of his brain warned him that it would be his last gasp. There was no air down here. Only blackness. Pitch, as sticky as nightmares.

*Stop. Stop this, or you will die.*

He calmed his movement, trying to ignore the pressure like a vacuum in his lungs and the sensation that he was about to slip into unconsciousness. He bent his knees and allowed his fingers to fiddle with his shoelaces.

*Maybe . . . Maybe if I can . . . untie . . .*

A greenish light appeared somewhere above him. Eli panicked, worried that he was already on his way out. Here was that lovely tunnel of which people so often spoke.

The glow came closer, moving lazily, like the phosphorescent head lantern of a deepwater predator — one with teeth as long as syringe needles.

From inside the green light, a soft hand stretched out to him, thin fingers straining forward. *Another ghost,* Eli thought. *Coming to take me away.*

# CHAPTER SIXTY-ONE

JOSIE WATCHED AS Eli shrunk away from her.

*What are you doing?!* she shouted at him silently, saving her breath for when she might really need it. Then, she realized that whatever he was doing, he may not be doing on purpose.

The salt water burned her eyes, but she forced them open. Muffled sounds of surf pounded her eardrums. As she stretched her arm farther, her shoulder popped. She almost screamed out her pain, but instead, she pressed her lips together, keeping the brine out of her mouth and throat.

The flashlight was beginning to flicker, the water finally working its way through the seams of the metal body. Down below, Eli went limp, his limbs like noodles. Josie knew he might have only a few seconds left.

Scissor-kicking closer to him, she saw the real problem: His sneaker was stuck in the crevice where they'd discovered the swastika button. Eli had already managed to loosen his laces; they drifted upward like strands of seaweed. His head drooped, unaware of her presence. Josie came around behind him and wrapped her arms around his chest, clasping him like a lasso. She placed her feet flat on the floor of the cave, avoiding the snare of the fissure. She bent her knees and then pushed up as hard as she could.

Thankfully, Eli rose with her. With her chin grinding into his shoulder, she glanced down and noticed that one of his feet was now bare. He'd left his sneaker behind.

Breaking the surface of the pool, Josie was surprised to find the ceiling only inches from the top of her head. She turned Eli over so that he was floating on his back. The flashlight had dimmed but provided enough light to reveal the cavern's exit. Just beyond the open gate, Josie watched Vivian and Cynthia cling to each other, their mouths open in relieved shock. Their cries bounced all around the last of the available air space in the cave.

Josie kicked toward them, dragging Eli along beside her. Once she'd made it through the doorway, Cynthia and Vivian clasped their children and helped pull them out of the tunnel. Around the bend, the stairway appeared. The number of steps had been significantly shortened by the rising tide. The enshrouded sky opened overhead. Josie's mind was flooded with so many thoughts and hopes and fears that she nearly stopped moving. But her mother eased her along, until she felt the soles of her boots scrape against the stone floor.

Josie nearly broke down when she turned to see Cynthia helping Eli crawl up the steps. He was conscious! He was moving as slowly as a slug, but that didn't matter. He was moving. *Thank you*, she thought. *Thank you, thank you!* Josie didn't even know who she was thanking. Soon the others would be thanking her — chastising her foolishness for risking her life, but thanking her nonetheless.

# CHAPTER SIXTY-TWO

BRUNO WAS ON the ground — eyes closed, breathing steadily — at the top of the steps. While Josie had been underwater, Margo and Aimee had managed to haul him up the stairs before the flood overtook him.

Soaking wet and shivering, Josie stared at her brother, remembering the moments that had led to them taking that tumble. The hug — his strong arms squeezing the breath from her lungs. Had the jolt to his head knocked sense back into him? When he woke up (if he woke up), would he be himself again?

As Cynthia fawned over Eli, who was lying a few feet away from Bruno, Josie tried to explain to everyone what she'd overheard when she'd crept to the fort. That the men had gone back to the house to look for her, that when she'd approached Bruno, he'd called out a warning to them. It was possible that they would return. Maybe they were watching right now. But everyone was crying, and Josie wasn't sure anyone actually heard her.

Aimee stroked Bruno's cheek, speaking quietly into his ear. "Wake up. Please, wake up. I know it wasn't you who did that. I understand everything. I'll try to forgive you. I promise, just wake up." Vivian joined her, kneeling at his side, holding his shoulders, trying to shake him into consciousness.

"We need to be quiet," Josie whispered. No one was paying attention. She stood, watching through the fort's doorway for any movement on the spit. But the flashlight finally died, and the slope went black. She laid the metallic tube on the ground next to

Eli's head and sat beside him on the stone floor. He glanced at her. Even in the dark, she made out his grin.

"My mom says you saved me," he said. Sitting across from Josie, Cynthia held his hand.

"If you hadn't been such an idiot, I wouldn't have had to," Josie snapped, not realizing until that moment how angry she was with him.

Cynthia nodded, her lip trembling. "It was a dumb thing to do, Eli. I don't know what I would've . . ." She trailed off, unable to continue.

"Please, Mom," Eli said, slurring speech. "Don't cry. I'm sorry . . ." He struggled to sit but only managed to prop himself up on his elbows. Cynthia raised his hand to her mouth and kissed it again and again. Josie felt warmth rush her own cheeks. She moved to stand, to go check on her brother again, when Eli reached out and grabbed her wrist. "Where were you before? We looked everywhere." Teeth chattering, his words poured out, rushing like water off a cliff. "The tree crashed through the solarium. And you were gone. And then we went upstairs. And my dad and the others thought they saw you way out here. And we followed them. But then they changed. And Gregory told us his name was Coombs. But he was a ghost. And he said Margo's mother lived on this island when she was a girl. And she was responsible for his death. And before we knew it, Bruno and Charlie and my dad and Gregory forced us —"

"I know," Josie answered, trying to speak over him.

"And I almost died! In the cave, I saw you swimming toward me with your light and I thought you were an angel or something coming to take me away. I was so scared."

"I know, Eli. I know." Josie reached into her jacket pocket, feeling the wet cover of Dory's journal. It was probably ruined now, the words on the pages blurred into nothingness. History erased. But that was the least of her worries. "I know everything. I promise, I'll tell you more, but first you need to help me."

"Help you what?"

"Convince everyone that we've got to find a place to hide. And quickly."

Gasps rose up from behind them. Cynthia, Eli, and Josie turned to see what the commotion was all about, but when Aimee shouted out "Bruno!" Josie knew exactly what she'd find. She stood and wandered over to where Margo and Vivian and Aimee were crouched. Bruno's eyes were open. He was staring blankly at the sky, blinking again and again. He didn't seem to notice the women leaning over him, nor their tears wetting his forehead like rain.

Josie saw what was coming a moment before it happened. She started to reach out toward the group, but she wasn't fast enough. Bruno raised his hands so quickly that Margo, Aimee, and Vivian didn't notice they'd all been knocked backward until they were lying on the ground.

Bruno swung himself forward into a crouch and struggled to rise. But after his initial burst of energy, he seemed to falter, his legs wobbling before he could make it all the way up. Falling to his knees, he called out weakly, *"Achtung . . . Achtung, meine Brüder!"* Bloody saliva oozed from his mouth and dripped down his chin. In the shadows, the spittle looked like ink.

*Brüder.* A word Josie definitely recognized. "Bruno!" she shouted. "You're *my* brother. No one else's. Stop this!"

He ignored her. Raising his hands to his head, he closed his eyes and wavered. He looked like he might pass out again.

Vivian rolled out of his reach. Rising to her feet, she took Josie's hand. *"That* is not your brother. Not right now." Aimee, Beatrice, and Margo moved away too, standing in a circle around Bruno, watching the groom-to-be as if he might burst.

*"Achtung . . ."* he whispered, unable to catch his breath. All the fight had gone out of him. Then he collapsed to the ground, falling unconscious again. Vivian knelt beside him and reached out to check his breathing.

"It's not safe here," said Eli, coming up behind his mother, steadying himself on Josie's shoulder. "Josie's right. We've got to move."

"And what about Bruno?" Aimee asked. "Do we just leave him here?"

The group glanced wordlessly at one another. They already knew the answer. They also knew they had no other choice.

# Chapter Sixty-Three

Beatrice led the way back across the spit, suggesting that they stay near to the cliff, that it was less likely they'd be surrounded if the men could only come at them from one side. But with the violent wind, they had to be extra careful not to step too close to the edge. After everything they'd already been through, none of them wished to end up pulverized on the rocks below.

The wall of trees darkened as they came down the slope. Josie and Eli kept watch for shadows that looked like they might be alive and dangerous. Missing one shoe, Eli was also careful to avoid pointed sticks and stones. The group remained close together as they walked the jagged path. "Maybe the men never heard Bruno's cry," Cynthia suggested. The others murmured their assent. The sounds of crashing waves and distant thunder kept their voices from spreading too far.

"We should stay *off* the main path through the woods," Beatrice suggested, taking Margo's arm, as if they'd recently become the best of friends. "I'm pretty sure I can lead us through the rough."

"And what happens then?" Aimee asked. "We can't go up to the house. Josie said that they'd gone looking for her there."

"We'll stay along the island's edge," Beatrice said. "If we can make our way to the wharf without being seen, maybe we can wait out the storm in the boathouse. Sonny should arrive close to dawn. At this point, that must be only a few hours away."

"Now there's a plan I can get behind," said Vivian. Everyone else muttered in agreement.

As they stepped into the cover of trees, Josie felt comfortable telling them her own story of how she discovered the secret ladder in the closet and what she found when she explored the attic. She removed the water-warped book from her pocket and showed the group, sharing the story that Dory had written in it, sparing no detail. It was still too dark to see if any of the writing had survived the dive to the bottom of the black pool.

When Josie was finished, the others chimed in, drawing connections to everything that had happened. Eli was impressed. The group was finally, almost totally in sync with his impressions of the island. They agreed that it was haunted. And they believed that the spirits had taken control of the men for a singular purpose: to destroy Dory Sauvage's daughter.

Unsurprisingly, Margo remained quiet throughout the journey.

As the trees grew sparse and the house appeared at the top of the hill, Cynthia spoke up. "Are you all right, Mrs. Lintel? What's on your mind?"

Margo sniffed, as if she were uncomfortable with the question. She glanced down as she walked, careful to avoid fallen branches and low-growing brush that might snag her damp pants. "I'm not sure I can put what's on my mind into words," she said. "Especially not around the children." Nervous laughter followed. "One thing I'm unclear about is the girl Josie and Eli said they saw upstairs. I saw her myself this morning, though I didn't get a good look at her face. I'd mostly been thinking about the cannibal folklore. Those stories seem almost quaint now.

"What I mean when I say I'm unclear about our vision of this girl — how she led Josie to discover the ladder and the attic and the journal — is that the girl cannot be a *ghost* like the men who drowned in that pit in the fort. She cannot be a *spirit* trapped on this island. Reason number one is that, well, we know she survived that night because she gave birth to me. And reason number two is that she is *still alive*, if not quite well, residing in a nursing home outside of Bangor."

# CHAPTER SIXTY-FOUR

"WAIT A SECOND," said Josie, stopping short beneath the dripping branches. Water splashed against her scalp, but she smoothed it away. "Dory Sauvage is alive?" Everyone else paused along with her, willing, for a moment, to catch their breath.

"Her married name is Dorothea Petit," Margo answered. "And she's gone by Thea for years and years. But yes. My mother is no ghost."

"Maybe the figure we saw in the house wasn't your mother," Eli said. "Maybe it was some other girl."

"But Dory's journal didn't mention another girl," said Josie. "I mean, other than the girlfriends, Esther and Betty. But they were older. It had to have been her."

Beatrice spoke up. "Not necessarily."

"How's that?" Vivian asked.

Beatrice shrugged. "All I'm suggesting is that, in this life, there are more things that remain mysterious to us than not."

"When it was happening," Josie added, "when we saw her, I kept feeling like the island, or something, was trying to communicate with us. Share its memories. It felt like I was watching a movie."

"How much longer 'til we reach the boathouse?" Aimee interrupted, as though she were pretending that the last ten seconds of talk hadn't happened.

"That depends on how important everyone else feels it is to answer all of our questions *right now*," Beatrice said. "I say we keep walking. If we circle the edge of the yard, we'll be there in no time."

Once they'd stepped out onto the lawn, there was nothing but the darkness to cover them from the house. To their right, a thicket of trees clung to the rocks that leaned out over the ocean. A sporadic breeze continued to spray what was left of the rain. They walked in silence, ducking their heads, trying to be as small as possible.

Eli kept part of his vision on Beatrice, who was right ahead of him; he focused the other part at the top of the hill. The dark house looked as ominous as the fort. He knew now that bad things could happen in places as glorious as a white marble mansion or as decrepit as an abandoned jail cell. His bones were like liquid, conducting the buzzing electricity that flowed from his brain. An ambush might come at any moment, from any direction. He felt ready to pop. Josie strolled up beside him, and his nerves dialed down a notch.

He couldn't stop thinking about the girl who'd appeared in Josie's room that day. The vision. If evil can sleep in a certain place, waiting for the right moment to strike, then maybe it stood to reason that the place would have a desire to vanquish that evil. And if Margo's presence on Stone's Throw triggered the old dormant malevolence to awaken, to seek revenge, maybe it also triggered something good as well.

The wharf and the boathouse appeared ahead, the silhouette of its two-story roof sloping sharply toward the water that crashed up from below, splashing little explosions of foam high into the air.

# CHAPTER SIXTY-FIVE

"Hold on," whispered Josie, throwing out her arms, stopping everyone behind her. Ahead, Beatrice paused and turned around. They were only fifty or so steps from the darkened building. "What if this is a trap?"

Everyone was quiet for a moment. Eli wondered, had no one considered this?

"A trap?" Vivian echoed. "You mean, like, they expected us to come here?"

"As far as we know, they all think that we're back in the cave," said Aimee. "Drowned."

"Josie's right," said Eli. "We can't rule out that they know we've escaped. They might have planned for this."

Beatrice sighed. "Well, we can't stay in the open. When the sun starts to rise, we'll be sitting seagulls."

"You mean ducks?" Aimee asked.

"I'm just worried that if we hide in the boathouse," Cynthia added, "we'll be cornered if they come after us again."

"But we'll only be in there until Sonny arrives."

"That could be hours!" said Aimee.

"If the storm calms down," Beatrice went on, "and if it's an emergency, we can always pile into the dinghy."

"The tiny boat tied to the wharf?" Cynthia asked. "That doesn't sound very safe."

"None of this is *safe*," said Beatrice. "That little boat may be our only hope."

"Why are you so determined to get us in the boathouse, Beatrice?" Aimee asked.

"I believe I just answered that question. Several times."

"But why should we trust you? You might be working for *them*. Your husband tried to kill Margo."

Beatrice scoffed. "And your fiancé attacked you! And then he helped lock us all in a flooded fort! You're really going to start pointing fingers?"

"Enough," Vivian whispered harshly. "Arguing won't help." She exhaled sharply. "You all stay here. I'll go check it out."

"Mom! No!" Josie cried out.

Vivian clasped her daughter's shoulders and squeezed. "It's not a big building. I'll search every corner. When you see me waving from the front door, you'll know it's clear."

"I won't let you go alone."

"I'll only be a few minutes, honey. Stay with Eli. Protect each other."

Josie glanced at Eli and then sighed loudly. Even now, Eli's skin tingled with embarrassment.

"There is another option," Margo said quietly from the rear of the group. Her voice was like a silver bell, ringing out for everyone's attention, reminding them that she was still with them. Everyone turned to listen. "I could go up to the main house. Alone."

"No way," said Beatrice. "We're almost out of this."

"*Almost out* leaves a lot of room for error," said Margo. "For unnecessary trouble. They want me. They want to hurt my family. They've no real interest in any of you. If we give them what they want, maybe they'll leave the rest of you alone."

"You're willing to sacrifice yourself for a *maybe*?" said Beatrice.

"Yes," said Margo simply. Her silence on the walk from the fort suddenly made sense to everyone. "I am."

"Don't be ridiculous," said Aimee, pushing through the crowd, taking Margo's hand, as though she could physically restrain her if she tried to break for the hill top. "You're not going anywhere without us."

Margo's lip trembled, and she choked out a strangled sigh. "This is all my fault."

"No, it's not," Josie spoke up. "This is nobody's fault."

Eli added, "I guess if you want to blame someone, you can blame Hitler." Margo sniffed. "He started that war. He sent the submarines. He did the most horrible things anyone has ever done on this planet."

"I agree," said Cynthia, squinting her eyes in anger. "Screw Hitler!" This made the entire group snicker reluctantly. Eli had never heard his mother use such language. He felt a sudden surge of pride for her. "What is it? What did I say?"

"Forget it, Mom," Aimee said. "You're just funny sometimes."

"I'm so sorry," Margo went on. "I had no idea about any of this. My mother never said —"

"Enough," Vivian said softly, waving her hands to cut her off. "Would it have made a difference if she had?" She didn't wait for an answer. "We will survive this, all of us, but only if we're smart about it." She stepped toward the boathouse. "Watch for me from the doorway."

# CHAPTER SIXTY-SIX

SEVERAL MINUTES LATER, Vivian was standing in the entry with her hands over her head.

All clear.

The group rushed the short distance to the boathouse. Vivian stepped aside, and everyone pushed past her.

As the lightning continued to flash, the first floor was revealed. The large room was filled with all kinds of equipment: fishing nets, stacks of folded canvas, coolers, small buoys. A statue of a mermaid leaned in one corner, her chest out, her arms at her sides. Josie recognized it as a prow figurehead. Maybe she had once guided a large ship across the water. On the opposite side of the room, a large green rubber raft was upended against the wall; dusty with age, it didn't appear to be the least bit seaworthy. Along the base of the same wall, several owls glared. Josie nearly screamed at the sight of their reflective yellow eyes staring hungrily at her before realizing they were plastic dummies to keep the seagulls away.

"There are guest rooms upstairs," said Beatrice. "A bathroom. Towels. Water. Beds. Clean sheets. We can relax."

"I'd be happy to sit down," said Aimee, "but there is no way that I can relax. Who will be the lookout?"

"We'll take shifts," said Vivian. "Or we can all do it together."

After they piled some of the junk from the storage area in front of the main doorway — a couple of chairs, a heavy toolbox, an upended table — the group climbed the stairs and settled into a single room that was situated at the southwest corner. Two windows had perfect views up the hill. If anyone were to approach the boat-house, he'd have to cross the great lawn. It was still dark out, but they'd surely notice any movement in the clearing.

Everyone gathered before the windows, watching intently for a few moments, before they started to feel crowded. Eventually, they took turns in the bathroom, washing up, drying off. Eli even managed to locate a pair of rubber boots that fit him.

"We made it," said Aimee after a few minutes. "I can't believe we made it."

"Back in that cave, I really thought we were done for," said Vivian.

"God bless you, Josie," said Cynthia. "Thank goodness you kept your wits about you."

Josie smiled and blushed. Soon, she felt wet streaks on her cheeks. "I didn't think about it," she said through her tears. "There wasn't any time. I just knew I had to act fast." She rubbed at the pocket of her jacket, feeling the edges of the book she'd discovered in the attic. She reached inside and pulled it out. "Margo, this belongs to you. To your mother. She was the real hero."

Margo sat away from the others on one of the beds and held the journal in her lap, staring at it in disbelief. She opened the cover and pawed at the wet pages, making out some of the words. The water hadn't completely destroyed the ink after all. "I can't believe this. I can't believe she kept it all from us, my brother and me, our entire lives." She flipped through the book. "I suppose the story explains her phobia of thunderstorms." She shook her head and then read a line aloud. "*If you're reading this, I'm probably dead*'?" She looked up at the group. "When she left this book in the attic, she probably did believe that the Nazi U-boat was going to come for them. She hid, but she thought there was a chance she'd be found, and not by the good guys. And if that had happened . . . Well . . ." She placed the journal on the mattress.

"I guess Dory never had a chance to retrieve her diary," said Eli. "I wonder why."

"It's like history loops around," said Josie, eyeing the book. "Seems like people up here love telling stories. Wouldn't Dory's experience have been the ultimate tale to share? How come her story never left the island?"

Silence filled the small space for a few moments. Then, Beatrice spoke up. "I have a confession." Everyone turned toward her, and she held up her hands in defense. "That came out wrong. It's got nothing to do with what's happened here tonight. Well, not *directly*. It's just . . . Charlie and I have been keeping a secret for decades. A secret about Stone's Throw Island that may answer Josie's question. I think now is the time to tell it. And I don't give a good-gosh-darn about the repercussions."

# CHAPTER SIXTY-SEVEN

"You see," Beatrice went on, "Charlie and I knew that the Germans had attempted to take over this island. We didn't know the particulars, and we certainly didn't know the history or name of the family who lived here at that time. According to the information we received, the navy fleet in Portland responded to a distress call. Shortly after they arrived, they sunk the enemy submarine that was just offshore.

"Of course, there was a cover-up. The government thought that if the public ever got wind that the Germans had come so close to a land invasion of North America, there would be panic in the streets. They shut down the story — paid off or threatened the family who'd lived here. Margo's family. The government took the island from them by *eminent domain* and used it as a lookout point until the end of World War II.

"Later, during the Cold War, the big house became a military communications post. The government used it secretly in this manner all the way through the late eighties, when Charlie and I came on board as the caretakers. By that point, the building had become quite run-down. Only a few officers worked here, and they had little to do. Our jobs were to phase them out and then watch over the place until the military figured out what it wanted to use the island for next. As you know, they eventually sold it to the financial people on the mainland. The rest is public knowledge."

Sensing the end of the tale, Eli spoke up. "So you and Charlie were like spies?"

Beatrice laughed. "Hardly. We were the most ordinary sort of folk. No great stories to tell." She glanced at Eli and Josie, a glimmer of apology in her eyes. "No secret children locked away in cages." She didn't pause to explain to the others what she meant. "It just so happened that the job we found was in an unusual place, working for an unusual group of people."

"To say the least," said Cynthia. "I can't imagine having to keep such a secret to yourselves."

"Back then, I couldn't imagine it either," said Beatrice. "But over the years, my imagination has grown. It's funny, when I first set foot on Stone's Throw, I knew there was something odd about it. Something off. Deep down, I think I believed that something as strange as this would happen one day. Like a bomb. Someone just needed to come along and light the fuse."

"Me." Margo shifted her weight, and the bed where she was seated squeaked. "I was the spark."

"Let's not start that again," said Vivian. "We're safe here now."

Aimee shushed them, pointing toward the closest window. "Are we really?" she whispered.

At the top of the hill, a few lights had emerged from the shadows by the big house's front door. They wavered wildly, like malformed and venomous lightning bugs. Seconds later, two spots, brighter than the others, appeared not far from the entry. These lights turned together and illuminated the wide expanse of sloping lawn that separated the house from the wharf.

Eli and Josie glanced at each other from opposite beds, their eyes wide. The men had rediscovered the golf cart.

# CHAPTER SIXTY-EIGHT

"No, no, no!" Aimee cried out. "How did they find us?"

"We can't be certain that they have," said Vivian.

"They're heading straight for us."

"That doesn't mean they know we're in here."

"They will soon enough," said Josie, standing and moving toward the bedroom door. The group followed her. "Maybe we should go downstairs and fortify the barricade."

"We can't stay in this house!" said Aimee, glancing back toward the window. The golf cart had come nearly a quarter of the way down the long path. "They'll do anything to get to us. I wouldn't put it past them to start a fire, burn us all alive."

"So what's your suggestion?" Eli asked. "We run outside to meet them instead?"

"Well . . . I don't know!"

"We can't just stand here," Josie said.

Margo raised her hand. "My offer stands. I can —"

Everyone answered at once: "No!"

"The little boat is still tied to the wharf," said Cynthia. "Maybe it's time to try that?"

"And do what, Mom?" Aimee asked. "Capsize offshore? Drown?"

"You're being very negative, Aimee."

"Negative? Are you freaking kidding me?"

"Either we end up back in the hands of the men," said Eli, standing by Josie, trying to keep his voice calm, "or we try our luck in the dinghy, where we at least have a chance to get away from them."

Josie nodded. "It's the only answer. Beatrice, do you know how —"

Beatrice didn't wait for her to finish. "Follow me," she said, pushing through to the doorway and heading down the stairs.

Josie noticed that Margo had left Dory's journal behind, so she picked it up and shoved it back into her pocket.

The glow of the headlights through the downstairs windows projected panels of white onto the ceiling and the walls of the storage room, sliding around like alien creatures searching for a place to hide. The group shoved away the makeshift barricade from the exit.

"Make sure everyone takes a life jacket," Beatrice instructed, gesturing toward a nearby crate that was filled with bright orange floatation devices. She grabbed a fat red lantern from a shelf over the crate and then threw open the door. The wind greeted the group again, breathing salty mist into their faces.

Outside, the lights from the descending cart were blinding. Eli raised his hand to shield his eyes. The cart's engine snarled. If the men hadn't known before where the group had hidden themselves, they surely did now.

Beatrice waved for everyone to follow her around the corner of the boathouse, toward the edge of the wharf. Two thick wood posts rose up from below: a ladder leading down to the angry surf.

# Chapter Sixty-Nine

Because of the storm surge, the tide was much higher than it had been the previous morning, making the ladder shorter and the dinghy closer to the deck.

Eli and Josie climbed down the slippery rungs and stepped into the aluminum vessel. It was not a very big boat, maybe sixteen feet. A pair of long oars lay across its three wooden benches. The bottom was filled with almost a foot of water. The two glanced at each other, another silent question passing between them: *Will we climb out of this thing together on the other side of the gulf?* Soon, they found themselves helping the others down the ladder. Turning back had become an impossible notion.

As Beatrice busied herself for departure, Eli discovered a large plastic jug floating in the water by his ankles, a thin white nylon rope running from its handle to the side of the boat. The top of the jug was sealed shut, and the bottom had been cut open. If he held the jug by the handle, he could scoop the water out of the boat. He worked quickly, trying to empty the deluge.

After untying the line from the front of the boat, Josie sat down beside Eli, who was still scooping out the water, and then looked toward the back, listening as Beatrice gave instructions to the other women. "Pull the buoys inside! Untie this! Loosen that! Disburse your weight. Watch out for the gas tank. Make sure the life jackets are tied tightly at your neck!"

Beyond the lip of the deck, the misty atmosphere at the top of the ladder began to glow brighter. The golf cart was coming closer.

Soon, the boat was drifting, unmoored, rocking violently in the surf, bobbing up and down like a carnival ride. Beatrice stood, ignoring the disturbance of the waves, managing to keep her balance as though her legs were made of rubber. Vivian held out one arm for support and, with her other hand, raised the fat red lantern. The glow at the deck grew brighter. Beatrice fiddled with the long handle that protruded from the front of the outboard motor before lowering the prop into the water. Then, she grabbed hold of a knob at the top of the motor and yanked it swiftly back, nearly hitting Aimee, who was sitting across from her. A long cord stretched out from the motor and a loud growling noise came from inside it and then sputtered out. Beatrice tried three more times before the engine finally came alive, vibrating the aluminum body that enclosed them.

Slowly, the boat began to move out into the night. Seated on the bench at the bow, Eli and Josie clung to each other for a moment, as a real brother and sister would, reaching awkwardly around their bulky orange life vests. Giant swells brought them up and down, up and down. Waves splashed up over the side of the boat, drenching everyone. Eli glanced over the aluminum edge. The ocean parted ahead of them, but the water level outside seemed high, too high. The boat was sitting too deep, and Eli realized why Beatrice had saved this option for a last resort. There were too many passengers. Josie must have noticed the same thing because she released him and reached for the plastic scoop. She leaned down and tossed out water even as, every few seconds, the breakers dumped more inside.

The wind assaulted them from every angle. When lightning flashed, the clouds were revealed, spinning tightly in the sky overhead. Eli considered that they were in a metal boat. What if lightning struck?

His mother was sitting on the bench behind him. He reached back and took her hand. She squeezed his fingers, putting on a brave smile. *Please, please, get us through this*, Eli thought, imagining that somewhere Dory Sauvage was watching and wishing them success.

# CHAPTER SEVENTY

THEY ONLY KNEW the direction in which they were headed by looking back at the island. The golf cart's headlights were a diminishing beacon, a constant point on the horizon.

Eli couldn't be sure but he thought he saw figures moving around on the wharf. His father, Charlie, and Gregory. Was it possible that Bruno was still out on the spit by the fort, dazed from his tumble? Despite what they'd done, he hoped they were all okay. And he wondered what would happen when they got back to the mainland. Would the men remember any of this?

As the dinghy puttered farther out into the roiling gulf, the island disappeared into the darkness. Eli and Josie shared the task of scooping out the water, but it didn't seem to help. The waves continued to toss them around. Eli's head was spinning. Josie gagged, dizzied at what felt like a maelstrom drawing them toward its center. The women were shouting to one another over the roar of the wind tearing at the ocean. "How do you know where we're going?" "Trust me!" "Sit down!" This went on and on.

After a long while, Eli noticed a glimmer way back behind them, toward the island. Were those flashlights on the water? He felt his stomach sink. He remembered the large rubber raft that had been upended in the boathouse's storage room. "Look!" he called out, pointing. "They're following us!" The group stiffened and released a collective groan.

"Never mind that!" Beatrice cried. "Brace yourselves!" She raised her arm sharply and pointed to her left. "Wave! WAVE!"

Eli glanced around as he tried to figure out what she meant. Wave? Wave at whom? And then he saw it. A swell ten times the size of the others rose up out of the darkness, curling at the top, ready to crash.

# CHAPTER SEVENTY-ONE

BEFORE HE KNEW what had happened, Eli was underwater again, spinning out of control. He flailed his arms and legs, trying to steady himself. Water shot up his nose, forced its way into his throat. He swallowed it down. Thick and salty. Immediately afterward, he gagged, nearly vomiting up the contents of his stomach, but he managed to hold his breath. In the swirling darkness, he clutched at the life jacket that hugged his neck and felt it pulling him in a certain direction. It could only be up. Right? He kicked his legs. Seconds later, he broke through the surface, gasping for breath.

He struggled to cry out. "Mom! Aimee! Josie!" His voice crackled with phlegm and salt water.

The sky lit up. A dozen feet away, in the negative space at the bottom of a swell, the bottom of the overturned dinghy gleamed silver. Eli watched as several heads popped up around it. He couldn't make out any faces. He swung out his arms, kicking his legs toward the capsized boat.

The momentum of the surf carried him forward. By the time he reached the others, they'd already managed to grab hold of the vessel. To his horror, the current pushed him past the dinghy. He tried to turn around, to swim back, but the ocean had already decided his fate.

The wind carried away the sound of screaming — the others', his own.

*This is it,* he thought. *I'm going to die.*

He was a dozen yards gone when something splashed right next to his head. He cried out in surprise and then instinctively grabbed at the object. It was white and hard. He recognized it instantly: the plastic scooper from the dinghy. As soon as he had a hold of it, he felt himself being slowly reeled back to the boat.

At the other end, he saw Margo and Josie working together to help him. They were each grasping the boat one-handed. When he was within a couple of feet, they reached out and caught his life jacket. He threw himself up onto the bottom of the boat, shuddering. "Thank you," he said. "Thank you, thank you." It seemed as though they were the only words he knew anymore.

"Are you okay?" Josie called out to him.

"No way," he answered, coming back into himself. "Are you?"

"Not a chance!"

Margo hung on to the vessel. Eli could hear her sobbing.

"Where are the others?" he asked. "My mom? My sister?"

At that moment, he heard another voice call to him from nearby. Pulling himself farther up onto the capsized dinghy, he caught a glimpse of the water on the other side, by the upended propellers. To his relief, he saw his mother's face. She and Vivian clutched at the edge of the vessel. "Mom!"

"Where is Aimee?" Cynthia cried out. "Where's your sister?"

# CHAPTER SEVENTY-TWO

ELI, MARGO, AND CYNTHIA dragged themselves to one side of the dinghy. Josie and Vivian held on to the other, trying to keep everything balanced. The waves continued to swell, bringing them up out of the valleys and then dropping them back down. At each crest, they scanned the black water within view, but they still had no sight of either Aimee or Beatrice. They shouted their voices to tatters, listening through the gale for an answer, but none came.

Eli's own mind raced. *We'll find them. We have to find them. Aimee is marrying Bruno on Sunday. The lobster people are coming tomorrow. I'm supposed to help everyone set up the seaweed platform for the bake. We're wasting time. This is so stupid!*

"I'm going to go search for her!" Cynthia said through a sudden mouthful of sea foam. She choked, hacking up whatever had slipped down her esophagus.

"Don't you dare let go," Vivian answered, her voice low and threatening. "Your son needs you, Cynthia!"

"But Aimee is out there!" Eli shouted. "Maybe she and Beatrice are nearby!"

"No!" Vivian called to him, slapping the belly of the boat that was now between them. It rang out with a hollow metallic thud. "This is how people die! Stay put. We cannot lose you too!"

"Help will be coming soon," Margo offered. "Let's hold on for just a little longer."

*Of course,* Eli thought. *Yes. Help. It will be coming. That's what happens in these kinds of situations. Right?*

Cynthia opened her mouth in a silent wail. Her blond hair was plastered to her face, making her look like a demonic creature crawling out of the dark water. A mermaid. A naiad. A siren. It made perfect sense. This whole day had felt like something out of a fairy-tale nightmare.

At the next crest, a flash of light greeted them from not far away.

"Hey!" Eli shouted, waving his hand as high and hard as he could.

"Eli, *shh*!" Josie said, shaking her head.

"What? Why? It's help! It's the help that Margo told us was coming!" Even as he spoke, he realized his mistake; the tumble into the ocean had confused him, momentarily scrambling his thoughts. Voices called back to them, but Eli couldn't make out any of the words. The other vessel slipped down the slope of a wave, casting a beam of light on the trough. When it reflected back up at the newcomers, their identities became clear. Charlie, Gregory, and Otis were in the large rubber raft, rowing toward them.

"This is *not* the kind of help we need!" Josie answered.

# CHAPTER SEVENTY-THREE

THE GROUP WATCHED in silence as the men came closer. *What to do? What to do?* The words were a gale inside Josie's skull. This rescue would put them right back into the hands of the men who'd attempted to drown them only an hour prior.

To let go of the boat would mean they would separate and possibly get lost in the gulf. But to stay . . . to stay . . .

The raft came closer, skiing down another steep swell. This time, when the men shouted out, Josie could hear what they were saying.

"Is everyone okay?"

"Stay where you are! We're coming to get you!"

And, "Cynthia! Cynthia! I'm so sorry, honey! Please answer me!"

Josie shook water from her face trying to focus.

The men sounded no different than they had early that morning, before they'd even set foot on Sonny's ferry. Had the spirits of the Nazi sailors departed? She wanted to shout out to them to go search for Beatrice and Aimee. The two couldn't be far. The rest of the party should be fine hanging on to the dinghy until everyone else was safely returned.

"They're here to help!" Cynthia said, lifting her body high up onto the underside of the boat. "Otis! Please! Hurry!" Everyone else remained quiet, unsure of the truth.

Eli tapped at the dinghy to catch Josie's attention. "How can we trust them?" he called out to her.

"This isn't right," she agreed.

Nearly twenty yards away, the men continued to row the rubber raft, keeping their flashlights directed at the overturned dinghy. "Almost there!" one of them called out. "Almost safe!"

Josie wondered when they'd notice that their group only numbered five. *Safe* seemed like a cruel word when two of them were still missing. Except for Eli, the others were now crying and shouting and waving, wanting to believe that none of what had happened earlier had happened at all.

When the raft was ten yards out, the men began to cheer more encouragement and apologies. Their faces were intermittently lit by their wavering flashlights, and Josie wondered if her fears were unfounded. They looked worried. Shocked. Weary. But as the distance closed between the vessels, the fact that no one had yet mentioned Aimee's and Beatrice's absence disconcerted Josie. Their headcount must be perfectly clear to the men at this point. Didn't Otis care that his daughter wasn't visible? Wasn't Charlie concerned for his wife?

"Come around this side of the boat," Josie called out to Eli. "Bring the others." When Eli squinted at her skeptically, she added, "Trust me! And hurry!"

Eli goaded Margo and Cynthia around the sharp props of the motor to the other side of the boat. They were confused and in shock, as was Eli, but they gave little argument. Josie and Vivian made room for them by sliding toward the bow. When they were all in place, Josie explained, "It's just in case the raft collides with us. On this side, we won't be crushed." What she didn't say, but thought, was, *On this side, it'll be harder for them to grab us.*

# CHAPTER SEVENTY-FOUR

WHEN THE RAFT was only a few feet away, the men reached out with their oars, trying to catch the dinghy and hold the two vessels together. Wood slammed against metal and rang out into the night, like a bell on a buoy.

"Come back around," Gregory said, holding out his hand. "We'll pull you up!" When no one moved, he smiled sadly, his brow furrowing. "I know this is an almost ridiculous request, but you have to trust us. We're here to help!"

"We're frightened, Gregory!" Margo cried out. "Beatrice and Aimee are gone! And . . . And we don't know who any of you are anymore!"

"We're *us*!" said Otis, kneeling and holding out his arms toward them.

Again, Josie thought, no comment about his missing daughter? And Charlie'd barely flinched at the mention of his wife's name.

"Where's Bruno?" Vivian asked.

"We couldn't find him back on the island," Gregory cried. "Come on! We've got to get you out of that water!"

"Gregory?" Vivian said. "You're sure that you're Gregory Elliott?"

Gregory's grin widened. "None other," he said.

To Josie's left, her mother pulled away, moving around the bow. Once Vivian made this decision, it would be made for all of them. Josie grabbed for her mother's life vest, but the orange nylon slipped away from her fingers. Vivian stretched her arm up toward Gregory's open palm.

Lightning. A crack of thunder. And in that second, Josie saw something in Gregory's face that sent her spiraling into panic. His skin had been sallow, pulled taught over a gaunt skull. His eyes had been empty sockets except for what looked like a crab claw reaching out from the one on the right, clamping down on his lower lid. His nose had been missing, nothing more than two tiny holes in the center of his face. Pieces of flesh had been torn away, revealing bloody bone and teeth. In that flash of lightning, Gregory had looked like a ghoul. And Josie knew: The hungry ghost of Emil Coombs was still wearing Gregory Elliott's body like a costume.

# Chapter Seventy-Five

"Mom! Wait! Stop!"

To Josie's relief, Vivian withdrew her hand and glanced over her shoulder. "What is it? What's wrong?"

Josie looked up at Gregory as he snapped his glare toward her. He knew that she knew. And he understood that this part of his game was over. He'd lost.

The others noticed his expression too. Vivian kicked backward from the raft so quickly, she almost lost her grip on the bow, but Josie grabbed her elbow and pulled her close. With one arm, Vivian hugged her daughter, crying out in shock at what had just happened.

"He's lying," Josie explained. "They're all liars!"

Eli leaned toward her. "You saw it too?"

Josie nodded, tears leaking from her eyes.

Instantly, the men changed. Gone were the helpful and worried expressions. They stood in their raft, staring down at the group huddled in the water, each smiling the same satisfied smile. Charlie and Otis raised the long wood oars, reaching out farther, almost over the heads of those bobbing in the surf.

If they brought them down, Josie thought, well . . . it was over. The only option left was to let go of the dinghy and drift into open water.

"Stop!" said Margo. "Hold your horses! I'm coming around. You can have me." Otis and Charlie paused, glancing at Gregory as if for orders. "On one condition. You must not touch the others!"

Gregory laughed. "You'll leave them here?"

"They'll have a better chance out here than with you, of that I'm quite certain." She struggled to move back around the stern of the boat, grappling the edges tenderly, avoiding the sharp propellers that were only inches from her face. "Just get this over with." Josie thought she could hear Margo chuckling to herself, as if something in her head had snapped. As if she had nothing left to lose. At this point, she'd crawled too far away for anyone to stop her. Josie understood that arguing would be pointless. "So, what do you say?" Margo went on. "Do we have a deal?"

"We do," said Gregory, reaching out again, this time for Margo's hand.

The sound of a horn blasted somewhere nearby. Momentarily forgetting the melodrama that was playing out before them, everyone turned to see where the noise had come from. To Josie's surprise, another light was approaching from the opposite direction. It cast a strange, wide beam that seemed to hover and sway across the pulsing waves, back and forth, until it finally settled on them. Then came another blast from the horn.

When the ship was within shouting distance, Josie's heart switched into high gear. She could just make out the words written on the bow. It was the *Sea Witch*.

# CHAPTER SEVENTY-SIX

"Hold it," Sonny Thayer said, clutching the ferry's wheel. "What's that out there?"

Rick stood beside him, directing the spotlight where his grandfather instructed. When he found the aluminum boat and a large rubber raft floating beside it, he steadied his hands. "Well, I'll be . . ." he whispered. "Gramps, you were right."

"Told you I was better out here than on the road."

Back at Haggspoint Harbor, when they'd discovered that the current had dragged the ferry upstream, Rick had begged Sonny to leave it alone. But Sonny wouldn't listen. He'd made his way to the end of the slip and hopped into the dinghy, insisting that they locate the ferry. When Rick realized that his grandfather was not going to take no for an answer, he followed, shouting out that the old man was going to get them killed. But they'd found the ship a half hour later, stuck loosely in a wet marsh a couple of miles inland. Sonny was so relieved, he didn't bother saying to Rick *I told you so*. The two of them had simply tied the dinghy to the stern, climbed aboard, and gunned the engine.

Later, in the gulf, Sonny asserted that he'd heard a distress call — a clanging sound that Rick hadn't noticed over the wind and the waves — and Sonny, being Sonny, had decided to track it down.

"But is that them?" Rick asked, shining the spot on the water. Every one of the group was looking toward the ferry with anticipation. "What on earth are they doing way out here?"

"Let's go see," Sonny said, throwing the throttle forward.

# CHAPTER SEVENTY-SEVEN

"HELP US!" JOSIE cried out. Without thinking, she let go of the dinghy and tried to swim toward the spotlight, but the current snatched her up, carrying her toward the darkness outside the spotlight's range.

Eli reached out. Catching her life jacket, he managed to drag her back to the capsized boat. "Don't get too eager," he said. Josie stared at him in shock, appalled at how easily she might have slipped away.

"Thank you," she said.

"I owed you one anyway."

They glanced at the men on the raft. The trio stood straight, somehow weathering the rocking of the vessel, staring at the larger boat with empty expressions.

Lights blinked on around the perimeter of the large boat, illuminating a thirty-foot radius of furious water. A figure appeared by the railing at its side.

"Hey!" Rick Thayer waved. "Hold on just a second longer." He disappeared for a moment, and when he returned, he concentrated on tying something to the railing. Soon, he flipped the object up over the rail. A rope ladder unraveled and dropped down. Then, Rick held up a white foam lifesaver ring. It was attached to a cord that trailed off behind him. "One at a time!" he said. "Catch!"

The first time Rick threw out the loop, Josie snagged it. She called out, "Margo!" Then she passed the flotation device down to the woman who was still clutching the upturned motor. Margo opened her mouth to argue but then seemed to realize that to do so would only waste more time. She hooked her arms through the lifesaver.

"Good," Rick called out. "Steady now!"

At the ferry, Margo struggled a bit climbing the ladder, but she made it to the top. Gregory and his crew watched silently from the raft.

In this way, the group made their way to the *Sea Witch*. Cynthia and Vivian insisted Josie and Eli grab on to the lifesaver together. They cried in disbelief as Rick reeled them across the water, away from the danger of the men on the raft.

Once on the deck of the *Sea Witch*, they gathered with Margo to help Rick pull in their mothers. Rick explained that Sonny was up on the bridge, struggling to keep the wheel steady. When Vivian climbed over the railing and onto the deck, the five survivors watched Rick glance tentatively out at the men, looking ready to toss the foam ring again. They all shouted, "Stop!"

Rick rocked back on his heels, shocked at their ferocity. Otis, Charlie, and Gregory continued to stand straight, staring up at the group at the railing. "Stop what?" asked Rick.

"Don't throw them the rope," said Josie.

"They're not who you think they are," said Eli at the same time.

"They're not?" Rick asked, peering quickly around at the rest of the group. The women shook their heads. Cynthia covered her face, heaving with sobs. "Then who are they?"

"It's a long story," said Margo, touching Rick's shoulder. "But the kids are right. We can't let them on board."

"Well, I don't think it's up to us anymore," said Rick, nodding at the raft. "Looks like they have their own plan."

The group on the *Sea Witch*'s deck watched as Otis and Charlie used the long oars to push away from the capsized dinghy's metal hull. The rubber vessel slowly floated in the opposite direction, riding at the crest of another swollen wave.

"Where are they going?" Cynthia asked, leaning forward, as if trying to reach out and stop them, as if she still had hope that things could be turned around.

Vivian sidled up beside her, enveloping her in a tight embrace. "It's for the best."

"We need to search for Aimee and Beatrice," Eli said.

"Search for . . ." Rick's eyes went wide. "Oh no, please don't tell me —"

"Our boat turned over," said Vivian. "We lost them."

Rick paused, observing each member of the group, as if in awe. "What were you doing out here?" he asked. When no one answered, he shook his head and turned toward the stairway that led to the bridge. "I'll go tell Sonny —"

The last piece of his statement was drowned out by a new sound, louder than the wind, the thunder, the ocean. It was a great droning — a humming, grinding sound, like a helicopter descending or a plane on a runway at liftoff. Josie and Eli glanced up and around, looking for some sort of machine coming at them from the sky.

They should have been looking down.

# CHAPTER SEVENTY-EIGHT

NEARLY FIFTY YARDS off the side of the ship, the ocean began to foam and roil in a massive white oblong patch. Moments later, an enormous black fin burst through the surface. Its tip was sharp like a blade, and it kept rising and rising, dozens of feet into the air. A tumultuous wake rolled away from it on all sides. The humming sound grew to a roar.

The ferry's passengers clutched rungs, poles, and railings to steady themselves from, at first, the surprise of the sight and then, a moment later, from the vicious rocking brought on by the wake.

Eli's first thought upon seeing the fin was that a massive pre-historic shark had marked them as a meal. It didn't seem so far off from everything else that had already happened that night. Only when the great fin tilted forward into the water — and a rectangular tower with spires and spikes mounted at the top emerged from behind it — did Eli fathom what he was actually observing: the ascension of a giant submarine.

Sonny appeared at the bottom of the stairwell, having rushed down from the bridge. No one even looked at him; they were mesmerized. "What in the name of all that's holy is going on out there?" he said.

Lightning jumped through clouds in the distance. For a moment, the sub was backlit, revealing a large group of men standing on the hull and simply staring at the ferry. "Who are *they*?" Cynthia asked. Another flash and it became clear that a large piece of the vessel was missing. Near the front of the platform where the crew had gathered, a jagged hole exposed the black innards of the ship. The submarine should not have been operational, yet there it was, its engine grinding away angrily somewhere deep inside the dark body.

With a subsequent lightning flash, for a horrific second, the true nature of these men became clear. Even from the distance at which Eli stood, he made out tattered uniforms, missing limbs, pale skin, hollow eyes staring back.

The ghost crew of a ghost ship.

Eli and Josie moved away from the railing and backed toward their mothers, who were leaning against the wall by the stairs. Beatrice's recollection hovered in Eli's memories: *The navy fleet from Portland sunk the enemy submarine that had been stationed just offshore.* This was that submarine. The U-boat. These were the rest of the men who had perished because of Dory's actions.

"We have to move," Josie whispered. "Now."

Sonny was in no state to listen. His jaw had dropped wide-open. From the vacant look in his eyes, his mind was off somewhere trying to make sense of what he was witnessing.

"Mr. Thayer," Eli tried, "you've got to get back up to the wheel. You have to turn this boat around!"

Cynthia broke away from the group at the wall and rushed forward to the railing. "Otis!" she cried. "No! Please!" Everyone turned to catch a glimpse of what she was seeing out on the water.

The rubber raft had come up alongside the U-boat's hull. The ghostly crew held out their skeletal hands toward the trio of men. Otis. Charlie. Gregory. The three reached up, claiming the help that was being offered to them. Before anyone else on the *Sea Witch* could shout an objection, the men climbed aboard the sub and stood with their compatriots, reunited in spirit at long last.

# CHAPTER SEVENTY-NINE

ELI RAN TO HIS mother's side and watched as Gregory, Charlie, and Otis descended into a hatch in the shell of the metal slug. Other members of the crew followed, one by one, until no one was left standing on the platform.

The sound of the ghostly engine rumbled ever louder. A halo of white surrounded the sub, millions of bubbles being released from inside. Cynthia hugged Eli, unable to watch. The platform where the crew had stood now vanished below the waves. A few seconds later, the rectangular tower went with it. Its spires and antennae were the last pieces to go, disappearing like skinny fingers waving a capricious farewell.

The empty rubber raft bobbed in the surf. For several seconds, no one on the *Sea Witch* said a word.

Vivian followed Sonny and Rick up to the bridge, trying to explain, as best she could, what had just happened. The others wandered the deck, holding on to the railing as the *Sea Witch* continued to sway under the spell of the immense waves, and peered out at the dark water. "Beatrice?!" they called out to the nothingness that surrounded them. "Aimee?!"

Every whitecap caught Eli's attention. Clutching the lifesaver, he'd rush forward only to realize he'd been fooled again. Though he'd seen his father go down with the U-boat, he continued to hope that he might spot him too. His stomach churned with dread — a dull pain that worsened with every second that passed.

He did not blame the men for what they did back on Stone's Throw Island. None of this had been their fault. And yet, he couldn't help thinking that each of their souls must have been cracked just enough to let in the bad spirits. Or maybe it hadn't been anything like that. Maybe Eli had merely been lucky that they hadn't crept inside of his own head too.

"Aimee?!" he called out, standing at the *Sea Witch*'s stern. "Beatrice?! Dad?!" Margo's voice echoed out in chorus with his mother's from the other side of the boat. Josie was ahead of him, leaning over the edge of the railing. Eli was about to turn around and search the waters off the rear of the boat, when he saw her flinch and then jump backward, surprised by something she'd seen. Turning to Eli, she motioned for him to come quickly.

Momentarily forgetting everything else, Eli dashed across the slippery deck. "What is it?" he asked. "What's wrong?" By the time he reached her, Josie had backed all the way against the cabin wall. A few feet away, the rope ladder was still tied to the railing, dangling over the edge into the water below. Her jaw was trembling. She raised her hand and pointed.

"Look down there," she whispered, nodding. "Tell me if you see anything."

"What are you —"

"Just look! I can't trust my own eyes anymore."

Eli edged toward the rope ladder. After everything that had happened, what could Josie possibly have seen to make her behave this way? The sub had sunk, taking the crew — taking his dad — with it. So what could be so scary —

A man was dangling from the bottom of the ladder. When he glanced up, Eli's throat swelled. He choked and then caught his breath again. Eli had seen this face before — when he'd been in the water beside the overturned dinghy. Here was the sallow skin, the collapsed nose, the empty eye sockets.

The crab that Eli thought he'd noticed earlier had either fallen out or had crawled farther in. "Gregory?" he said quietly, his voice wobbling on the dying wind. "Is that you?"

# CHAPTER EIGHTY

THE THING CHUCKLED as it took another rung, dragging itself fully out of the water, dangling from the ladder. It was still several feet below the deck, but Eli had a feeling it wouldn't remain that way for long. "Wrong," said the specter. The voice was a husk, a wrecked wrinkle of a whisper. "Gregory is down below now. With my crew." His forehead screwed up in disgust. "How many times must I ask you to call me Coombs?"

Eli felt Josie lean over the railing by his shoulder. "Agent Coombs," she whispered. "Emil."

"That's quite familiar of you, young lady," said the specter. "Some might even say rude."

"Rude?" Josie blurted out a guffaw, forgetting her fear. "I'm from Staten Island. I know *rude*." She began to tug at one of the rope ladder's knots that Rick had tied to the railing. She glanced at Eli, and he started to work on the other knot. "You haven't seen *rude* yet, buddy."

The specter reached toward her. "I wouldn't do that if I were you."

"Oh yeah?" said Josie. "Gimme one reason."

"Because if you send me away, I can't offer you the prize."

Josie and Eli let go of the knots, holding their hands over the railing as if they'd just learned they'd been playing with a bomb.

"Prize?" Eli asked. "What prize?"

The specter reached for another rung, pulling himself farther up the ladder.

"Stop right there!" said Josie. Coombs ignored her and clasped the next rung with his wasted fingers.

"What are you offering?" Eli asked.

"Are children nowadays really this dim-witted?" Coombs answered. "*What am I offering?* Why, your father, of course. Your father, and Charlie, and good old Gregory Elliott."

Eli felt faint. The boat rocked sharply and he stumbled forward, tilting over the rail. Josie grabbed his arm and yanked him backward. He shook his head and then focused on the nightmarish face below. Were Aimee and Beatrice part of the bargain too? "You'll . . . you'll give them back?"

"For a price."

Eli felt his lungs squeeze tight.

"Margo," Josie said. "You still want Margo."

The specter nodded. "All it would take is a little push at the right moment. Then, plop, into the drink. Down into the deep. With the rest of us." Voices called from the other side of the ship. Cynthia and Margo continued their hunt for Beatrice and Aimee.

"How can we trust you?" Eli heard himself ask. His body felt strangely weak, as if his skin were turning to mist.

"Eli?" Josie said, staring at him, horrified. Shaking her head, she turned away. "If you want Margo so badly, why don't you just climb up here and get her yourself? Or can you not do that anymore, now that Gregory is down in your sub?"

"Ahh," said the specter, his torn lips pulling back into something not quite resembling a grin. "Finally, a clever response. Two plus two equals four, does it not? And a spirit needs a body to have any effect on your plane. That's where you come in."

"But how can we trust you?" Eli repeated, feeling tears welling in his eyes. "How do we know that you can even do what you say?" He felt Josie squeeze his shoulder. When he glanced at her, his lip began to tremble. "My father is down there," he whispered to her.

"I know he can be awful sometimes. *Most* times. But he's the only father I have. How can I let him go? How can I let any of them go?"

"This is not your choice, Eli," Josie answered, slowly shaking her head. "It's something that's beyond our control. Like storms. Like wars. Like weddings." Eli glanced around the deck, trying to locate Margo. Josie clutched his forearm, forcing him to make eye contact. "The others may be gone, but we're still here. You and me. We're together and no matter what happens, we'll always be family."

"You can toss her over too, Eli," Coombs chortled. "Come on. Help out an old man . . . A very, very old man."

"You're not a man," said Eli, peering over the railing. His skin and muscle and bones ached in a way that reminded him he was made of solid matter. He planted his rubber boots on the floor to prove it to himself. "You never were. You were never even *human*. You were a monster when you were alive, and that's what you will always be. You're not going to take anyone else down with you. Not me, not Josie, and especially not Margo."

He grasped the knot at his fingertips and tugged. Josie saw what he was doing and immediately joined him. Within seconds, the rope slipped away from the railing and dropped into the water. A splash sounded below. Eli and Josie peered over the edge.

Coombs's head was just visible above the surface of the water. His hollow eyes stared up at them. Just before he was swept away into the night, he shouted out, his voice like a rumble of distant thunder, "Suit yourselves."

# CHAPTER EIGHTY-ONE

ELI AND JOSIE STEPPED back from the edge, looking at each other with panic. "Margo," they said at the same time.

Josie took Eli's hand and pulled him toward the bow of the ferry, rushing past the rows of benches that were bolted to the hull. They found the wedding planner standing in the crook of the railing at the very front of the boat. She was leaning forward, scanning the water for Beatrice and Aimee. Up on the bridge, Rick was swinging the spotlight back and forth across the waves. "Hey!" Josie called out.

Margo turned around, her eyes expectant. "You kids see anything?"

Eli imagined a pair of hands reaching up over the lip of the boat and grabbing her ankles. "Would you come here for a minute?" he said, trying to keep his voice calm. He only wanted to get her away from the edge.

"Everything okay?"

"Everything is fine," said Josie, her jaw set forward.

"Doesn't look like it." The bow dipped into the valley of a wave, striking the water. Spray came up high over Margo's head and rained down upon her. Grasping the railing tightly, she didn't seem to notice. "Looks like you both just saw . . . well, now it just sounds *stupid*, but it looks like you saw a ghost." She finally stepped toward them, and Eli exhaled his relief. He and Josie held their hands open to her. She paused and then tilted her head in confusion. "You two hear that? Listen."

The three met before the front bench. "I don't hear anything," said Josie. "Nothing besides the boat and the wind and the . . ." Her face went slack and she glanced back and forth between Eli and Margo. "Oh no."

"Oh no, what?" Eli asked.

"*Suit yourself,* he said," Josie whispered, glancing toward the water off each side of the bow. "Eli, Coombs isn't done with us yet. We told him *no*, but he's not giving up." She focused on a single spot in front of the boat and raised her hand. "There!"

That's when Eli noticed the white oblong patch appearing on the surface of the water not far ahead of the ferry.

Josie turned and ran toward the stairwell that led to the bridge. "Sonny!" she called out and then climbed the stairs. "Turn the boat! Turn the boat now!"

# CHAPTER EIGHTY-TWO

MARGO GRABBED ELI'S shoulders as the ship's weight shifted sharply. Together, they spun around and fell onto the closest bench, sitting and facing forward as if ready to look out for whatever was coming. Sonny must have already seen the bubbling area spreading out; he must have already been getting ready to react when he'd heard Josie's plea. Eli clutched at the seat beneath himself, knowing that if the rising submarine careened into them, there would be nothing to hold on to that would save him.

"Eli!" Cynthia approached from the other side of the ship, clinging to the outside wall of the cabin. "Margo! What's happening?"

"Sit down, honey!" Margo called out. "And hold on!" Cynthia dove atop the last row of benches, laying her body flat, wrapping her thin arms around the seat.

The patch of froth was off the bow to the right. The humming sound vibrated the air. What was left of the rain and the spray shimmered in the glow from the ferry's lights. Then, as before, the sharp prow of the U-boat broke through the surface, climbing into the air like a fish scrambling to jump out of the water. It came up fast, with a deafening roar, missing the ferry by what seemed like only several feet. Eli watched in awe as details of the rusted hull rushed by. They were so close he could make out the individual rivets that the Germans had once used to build these vessels in their secret factories before the war.

Sonny gunned the engine so that, as the U-boat began to level out, the finlike prow was near the ferry's stern. The wake pushed the *Sea Witch* sharply away, aiding its turn back toward Haggspoint Harbor.

Far off, on an invisible horizon, Eli thought he could make out the twinkling lights of the small town. At that moment, those lights looked to Eli like they might belong in heaven, they were so beautiful. As the ferry circled around, away from the U-boat, Eli took Margo's hand. "Are you okay?" she asked.

He thought about what the specter of Agent Coombs had requested. If they'd given him what he wanted, maybe they would be safe now. Or at least safer. Maybe Coombs wouldn't have sent the submarine to attack. But, Eli knew, none of that mattered. "I am if you are," he answered, his face burning with shame, feeling as if he'd just told her a lie, though he was pretty sure he hadn't. He turned around. "What about you, Mom? You all right?"

Cynthia returned a muffled reply that he took for an affirmative.

"Sonny will get us home," Margo said, sounding like she was trying to convince herself as well as Eli. "He's a good driver."

*A good driver?* He'd need to be better than merely good. Eli swallowed down his worry and nodded. Better not to think about anything else right now. Better not to imagine that they were leaving Beatrice and Aimee behind. Better not to imagine the specter of Coombs and his last words: *Suit yourself.*

# CHAPTER EIGHTY-THREE

THE *SEA WITCH* RACED for the shore, cutting through the white-caps like scissors through wrinkled silk.

Cynthia had worked up enough courage to release the seat of the bench she'd been lying on to crawl forward and join Eli and Margo at the front. It seemed too dangerous to make any further move.

Eli swiveled his body around, throwing one leg over the bench so that he could see what was in front of the boat as well as what was coming up from behind. He caught a glimpse through the window of the small group up on the bridge — Josie and Vivian stood behind Sonny at the wheel, hugging each other tightly. Rick clutched the spotlight, which was attached to the control panel to their left. Everyone looked as terrified as Eli felt.

Then he spotted the large shape behind them. The U-boat was giving chase. It looked like it was as far away as the length of the Olympic-size pool at the YMCA back home. The *Sea Witch* was clocking swiftly along, but the sub was keeping pace.

If the Germans had torpedoes, Eli wondered, would they be too old or deteriorated to detonate? After a moment, he concluded that the rules of technology were no longer in play. An ancient U-boat with a crater in its hull had risen from the ocean floor. He held his breath, waiting for a blast that might come at any moment.

The humming groan grew louder, vibrating the atmosphere as well as Eli's insides.

The clouded sky had begun to turn the slightest bit gray. Dawn was coming. Land was directly ahead. They couldn't be more than a mile from the harbor now, but at this speed, they'd reach Haggspoint's rocky outcroppings long before that. Eli wasn't sure if this was a good thing.

He turned back to find that the U-boat was nearly upon them. The finlike prow approached their stern like the tip of a butcher knife. With a screeching howl, metal scraped against metal, and the *Sea Witch* jolted forward. Margo yelped. Cynthia wrapped her arms around Eli's neck.

Dark pines appeared through the misty atmosphere in the distance — one of the tiny, uninhabited islands that surrounded Haggspoint. Was Sonny *trying* to steer for it?

The boat shuddered, then the stern seemed to rise up. Eli tried to glance back toward the U-boat, but some force — another rogue wave or the ghostly ship that was chasing them — bounced the three passengers onto the deck. He found himself rolling toward the edge of the bow. Throwing his arms and legs out, he managed to stop his momentum, and he skidded to a halt just inches from the railing. Margo and Cynthia lay a few feet away.

The *Sea Witch* was tilting forward sharply now, lifted up by the nose of the submarine, its bow dipping dangerously close to the surface of the water. The pines were coming up quickly. Too quickly. Surf gleamed white as it splashed against sharp rocks.

Eli struggled to stand, his feet slipping out from underneath him. He scrambled toward his mother and Margo, who'd managed to crawl back toward the benches. "We can't stay out here." He pointed up at the bridge, where Sonny was struggling helplessly to turn the ship away from its doomed course. "We've got to get inside."

The three held on to one another, hands linked like a loose daisy chain, and then dashed across the deck. At the stairwell, Eli nudged the others forward before following them up the steps.

When he reached the top, Josie turned from her mother. She

reached out toward him, as Eli watched the island approaching through the window. The land loomed large as the boat tilted even farther forward, lifted impossibly by the corpse of the once sunken U-boat.

Rocks leaped toward them like snapping teeth. Peering into Josie's eyes, Eli felt an odd calmness. He was about to take her hand when Sonny shrieked, "Down! Everyone get down! We're gonna hit!"

# CHAPTER EIGHTY-FOUR

IF SOMEONE IN those early morning hours had been watching from shore as the *Sea Witch* collided with the coastline of that nameless islet off Haggspoint, what he witnessed would have been burned into his memory forever.

It wasn't just the boat accident that had been so remarkable. Yes, the bottom of the ship had been torn away like the lid of a tuna can — as one would have expected during such a crash. Moments afterward, the vessel turned, spinning onto its side, scraping along the rough beach with a wrenching squeal. Glass shattered; glistening shards disappeared into the pines where the forest met the ocean. Seconds after that, a great boom sounded — the engine exploding — and then, black smoke began to swirl out from the twisted mass of steel that moments earlier had been the hull. All of these sights would have impressed even the most jaded of New England souls, but what made the accident even more spectacular was the long metal tube that had halted just offshore where the rocks rose up from the water.

It had been an alien-looking thing. From the way it seemed to sit and stare at the wreckage, one might have briefly imagined that it was alive. But when it let out a raucous wail, and began to back away into the roiling waters, any witness would have concluded that it was another vessel, an odd type of submarine, something the likes of which hadn't been in production for a very long time.

The strangest part of all: Before the submarine had a chance to submerge, the vessel appeared to become transparent, like a dense patch of fog. And when an enormous gust of wind whipped up, seemingly out of nowhere, the ship appeared to disintegrate. Whatever was left of its suddenly incorporeal body was carried away instantaneously, like mist, into the sky over the Gulf of Maine and beyond.

# CHAPTER EIGHTY-FIVE

IN THE EARLY HOURS of the morning after the storm, the coast guard received a distress call from the house out on Stone's Throw Island. A young man was claiming that his family and friends were missing. There were supposed to have been ten people with him on the island — a wedding party, he explained. But he'd awoken that morning to find himself completely alone. When authorities asked him for details, he professed that he had no memory of the previous afternoon and evening. He assumed that he'd hit his head. A tree had fallen on a portion of the house, and he was worried that some of the party had been injured.

As the coast guard was gearing up a helicopter to fly out and investigate the island, they received another report from the Haggspoint Police Department of a boat having collided with one of the rock shoals just outside of the harbor. The guard deployed a ship to this second scene to meet up with the police boat that had already traveled there.

# CHAPTER EIGHTY-SIX

As NEWS SPREAD about the crash of the *Sea Witch*, everyone in Haggspoint came to the same conclusion: What happened had been a miracle. Five passengers, the first mate, and the captain had all survived.

They'd been taken to the emergency room at Seward General, where they were treated for abrasions — nothing serious, nothing that required more than a few X-rays and a dozen stitches total.

# Chapter Eighty-Seven

By the time the sun had risen several inches over the quickly clearing horizon, the coast guard had arranged a wide search of the gulf that separated Haggspoint from Stone's Throw. Purportedly, of the ten members of the party that had gone out onto the waters during the storm, five were still missing. Three men and two women, including the bride-to-be. Several boats and helicopters circled the area for the entire day, even scouring some of the uninhabited islands, looking for castaways.

They had no luck.

# CRYSTAL SKIES

# Chapter Eighty-Eight

A MONTH AFTER the events of early September, there was a single question that Margo Lintel still struggled to answer: *What now?*

Thankfully, she had a shoulder to lean on whenever she was feeling particularly sensitive. For weeks, her brother, Robert, had been staying in her guest bedroom, even when she stubbornly insisted she no longer needed him. The truth was, Margo did need him. But she didn't want to be a burden. In fact, her greatest wish was to never burden another soul with the problem of her existence for as long as she lived — not her brother, not her ex-husband, not anyone.

Five people had been lost. Charlie and Beatrice. Otis and Aimee. And, of course, Gregory, her assistant, her partner — all of them victims of circumstances for which Margo would forever feel guilt. No one would ever be able to convince her otherwise.

When Robert had picked her up from the ER after that horrible morning, she'd learned that her worries about her mother had been unfounded. Thea'd never had a chance to fret about the thunderstorm. She had suffered a stroke shortly after the wedding party departed Haggspoint Harbor for Stone's Throw Island. Weeks later, their mama was still unconscious.

The siblings visited Thea together whenever they could, usually in the evenings. Margo would sit with her mother, holding her hand in silence with Robert at her side. But whenever Robert gave them privacy, Margo would share her own tale of Stone's Throw Island. Margo knew that her mother most likely could not hear her, but talking about the events, even to deaf ears, seemed to lighten the burden.

While Robert was at work, Margo would walk to the library in town to see what new romance novels had arrived, or she'd stop by the organic grocery store for a special, fresh-squeezed green juice. Since the incident, she'd asked Robert to reach out to her clients, cancel her engagements, and offer refunds. She couldn't imagine answering any emails herself or speaking with any happy couples about future plans.

*What now?*

Sometimes, on sunny autumn afternoons, she'd stroll to the beach and stare out at the water, allowing the soft sound of the surf to clear away unwanted thoughts.

In the first week of October, Margo received a small package in the mail. When she noticed the return address, she became nauseated. She knew that one of the families would reach out one day, but she'd hoped it wouldn't happen so soon. The bubblelike handwriting on the padded envelope and the postmark from Staten Island gave Margo an idea of what she'd find inside: a message from the girl. Josie. She gathered up all of her courage and tore away the flap. Upending the parcel over the kitchen table, she watched a water-damaged book fall from the envelope.

At first, she didn't understand what she was looking at. Only when she'd read the brief note — *Hi, Mrs. Lintel, This belongs to you. XO* — did the sight of the object begin to bring back memories.

# CHAPTER EIGHTY-NINE

ONE OF THE THINGS Josie liked best about autumn was the color of the sky. On cloudless days, the dome that sheltered the city was a shade of blue so pure that it made her think of bells ringing. Whenever this particular blue lingered overhead, the air cleared. Staten Island stopped stinking of garbage and sweat, and the yellow fumes that sometimes hung over New Jersey seemed to dissipate.

It was perfect weather for running. Whenever Josie began to feel overwhelmed by memories of Maine, she would slip on her special new sneakers and just go. Around and around the block.

On an afternoon in mid-October, after school had let out for the day, Josie was doing just that. After the third loop past her driveway, she finally broke a sweat. She didn't time herself anymore like she had whenever she'd run with Lisa. Time wasn't as important now — or speed wasn't, rather. *Time* itself felt more precious than ever.

A couple of weeks after returning home from the island, Josie had sent Eli a handwritten letter, and she was still waiting for a reply. At first, she worried that maybe the people from the government had intercepted her writing and were considering how they would punish her family for breaking the promise they'd been forced to make. This promise was why she'd stayed away from email, away from her cell phone, away from texting and messaging, where people with the right technology could steal a look at whatever she had to say. Though it was still risky, a letter had seemed like the safest way to reach out. But with every passing day and no response — not from Eli, or the government agents who had interrogated them in the wake of the tragedy — Josie figured that the only thing interrupting the communication was his reluctance to write back.

She didn't blame him. She couldn't imagine what he must be feeling. If she'd lost her father and her sibling like he had, she wasn't sure she'd be able to get out of bed ever again. And on top of that, the fact that he'd have to tell anyone who had questions the vague story that the agency had invented for them, instead of the truth . . . *When a dangerous storm suddenly threatened to flood the wedding venue, the entire party thought it best to escape to the mainland, but they'd been overcome* . . . well, it was enough to make Josie boil. But the people from the agency had promised that no one would be prosecuted for what had happened on the island if they all kept their mouths shut. Everyone understood that this meant *Bruno* wouldn't be prosecuted, and despite what they'd seen him do, they knew he should not be held accountable for his actions. If Eli was simply trying to protect Josie's brother, how could she possibly be hurt by his silence?

Fourth time past her driveway. Sun was starting to set. Josie picked up the pace.

At night, she worried about her brother. She worried about her mother. She worried about Eli and Cynthia and Margo. And Sonny and Rick Thayer and their broken *Sea Witch*. She'd thought sending Dory's diary to the wedding planner might quell some of her worry, but Margo had not replied either, and that had only jump-started another cycle of panic. Would things ever feel the same again?

Six times around. Seven. Eight.

She wished she could talk to someone about her storming thoughts. They were as frightening to Josie as the nightly dreams from which she woke, screaming in alarm. The following mornings, when the sky turned that bell-tone blue, Josie managed to push the nightmare away into the ghostly world of her memory and imagination, where the island rose up from the wicked ocean like a bastion in the darkness.

"Josie! Dinner!" Her mother was calling to her from the stoop of their brick colonial.

At the end of the block, Josie dropped away from her sprint, slowing to a brisk walk as she continued toward her house. She waved at her mother to let her know that she'd heard.

When she reached the steps that led up to the front door, her mother smiled. "I made spinach lasagna."

"Thanks, Mom," Josie said, trying to catch her breath. "Nice of you." *Ha*, she thought, wiping her forehead with her arm, realizing how a tiny thing like the prospect of a favorite meal with your family could make you forget, for just a moment, everything else in the world. She chuckled, feeling the cool air blow in from behind her, sending chills across her warm skin. Gather up enough of these moments and maybe —

"A letter came for you today," said Vivian, stepping aside, holding up her arms as if trying to avoid touching her sweaty daughter. "I put it on the table next to your plate. Open it after you wash up."

# CHAPTER NINETY

*Dear J —*

*Sorry it's taken me so long to write back to you. Things here have been really weird. Mom's been sad, and I have been too. I miss my sister and my dad. And every time I remember that you and me are not going to be "in-laws" anymore, I get even sadder.*

*I'm glad to hear that your mom is doing okay. And I'm sure Bruno will keep getting better every day. With your help, they'll survive. That's how it works, isn't it? I mean, that's how Dory and her brother, Frankie, must have gotten through it, right?*

*I'm still trying to figure out what really happened. Parts of it feel like a dream. And other parts . . . well, I still have scars as proof that I was awake. Getting your letter in the mail was like discovering a new bruise. I'm glad you sent it, but I was surprised. Those people told us —*

*Well, you already know what they told us.*

*I'm not sure how much you know about what else has been going on up here. The coast guard called off the search for the sunken you-know-what. And along with that, they've finally declared that "the missing" are now "casualties," even though they never found any of them. It's hard to think of Aimee and Dad like that. It's beyond unfair.*

*Now my mom actually has to start planning services, and I'm totally sure that she's nowhere near ready to do that. When we have dates, I'll let you and your family know. Do you think you'll be able to come up to Maine again? I wouldn't blame you if you didn't want to, but it sure would mean the world to us. To me. :)*

*I've been thinking a lot about the wedding that didn't happen. If I hadn't been so worried about how I was supposed to fit in to everything,*

*I probably would have looked forward to it. But I hadn't been looking forward to it. Not really. I remember thinking that it would be just another meaningless ritual. As if it were supposed to be magical. Say the words, and poof!*

*Ever since that weekend, I've been thinking that if people wish to be together forever, they should have to fight for it. They should be forced to survive something like we did. I bet there would be a lot less weddings in the world, but the ones who actually make it through the trial, the ones who live, well, you could probably be pretty sure those will be the relationships that last.*

*Maybe I'm wrong, but I think the same thing might be true about friendships.*

*I feel like us two are going to know each other for a very long time.*

*Write back soon.*

*Love your (almost) brother,*

*E —*

# CHAPTER NINETY-ONE

THE NIGHT THAT Margo received Josie's package, her brother drove her to the nursing home.

As usual, Margo held her mother's hand, lightly caressing her papery skin, feeling her mother's swollen veins rolling around beneath her fingertips. When Robert left to use the restroom, Margo removed the journal from her purse and placed it on the mattress. To her surprise, Thea twitched, as if shocked by static, and bumped her hand against the book's spine.

Margo leaned forward and whispered, "I brought you something, Mama." Then, without really understanding why, she slid the journal underneath her mother's pillow.

The next morning, when the home called, Margo had been expecting it; however, she never thought she'd hear the nurse say, "We've got some good news."

Robert and Margo rushed over to find Thea sitting up in her hospital bed, watching as they came through the door, looking like she'd anticipated them arriving at that exact moment. They cried out in joy and hurried across the room, embracing their mother carefully, as if a forceful jolt might just send her away again. The staff had told them that the likelihood of a recovery — especially from someone their mother's age — was close to zero. But there she was, once more defying the odds.

After the nurses filled the siblings in on Thea's state of being, her vital signs and such, Robert and Margo sat with her and shared stories of the past month — innocuous things like the unseasonable warmth, the exceptional foliage, the new stoplight in the center of town. They stayed away from any talk of what Margo had gone through. After about half an hour of this, Thea asked Robert if he wouldn't mind going out to the pharmacy to get her favorite brand of hand lotion. When he responded that he could bring it to her some other time, she insisted that he leave now.

As soon as he'd gone, Thea took Margo's hand. "I had a dream about you," she said.

Margo felt the blood drain from her face. "Did you really, Mama?"

"When I was asleep, I dreamed you were in trouble in the old house."

"Which old house is that?"

"You know which house."

Margo felt a rush of cold. "But, Mama, you never told me about —"

Thea went on, "You were with a whole bunch of people I'd never seen before, and you were all in danger. There was a little girl staying in my bedroom, and in the dream, I was a little girl too. I wished I could tell her to warn you, but I was stuck. I couldn't speak. The only thing I could do was remember. I knew if I showed the girl my memories, that would help *you*." Thea reached under the thin covers and removed the book that Margo had slid beneath the pillow the previous night. She held it up, her hand wobbling. Her gummy eyelids overflowed with tears, and her voice hitched. "I helped. Didn't I?"

Margo felt herself beginning to crumble, but she forced herself to sit up straight. She slowed her breath. And when she spoke, her voice was steady, as still as the water of the bay during that morning she'd traveled with the wedding party out to Stone's Throw Island. "Yes, Mama," she said. "You helped."

# ACKNOWLEDGMENTS

Thank you, as always, to my friends and family for helping me get to the finish line once again.

My uncle, Irv Piehler, pointed me in the right direction regarding the German conversations. Nadja Hemingway came along and helped clean up my royal mess. *Danke schön*, Irv and Nadja!

Gail Paradis-Avlas and Gail Roe provided much nautical guidance. The characters would never have gotten off Stone's Throw Island without their help. Bow? (Arrow?) Stern? Fore? Aft? (Before? After?) Dinghies? (Dingoes?) Who knew it was all so complicated? Any errors (and I'm sure that there are errors) are entirely my own.

Kevin Wolfe was gracious enough to allow me use of the super-powered, crime-fighting, invisible dolphin that we created while visiting Turks and Caicos together — a character so stupidly brilliant, she deserves to be on television, no? (Pay attention, Hollywood — low budget cash cow, up for grabs!)

Shirley and Perrin Harkins invited me to the most beautiful wedding ever at Wolfe's Neck Woods State Park on Casco Bay. Thank you both for introducing me to the magical wonderland that is Maine. Daniel Villela and my mother explored the islands off the coast of Portland with me . . . in the pouring rain . . . and it was awesome.

Barry Goldblatt is a wonderful agent. Nick Eliopulos is an editorial wunder-man, if that's a thing. Antonio Gonzalez knows how to coordinate the heck out of a school visit. Christopher Stengel's vision is constantly inspired. Shane Rebenschied is a magician with a ghostly paintbrush. Nancy Mercado, David Levithan, Brooke Shearouse, Rebekah Wallin, Erica Ferguson, Lori J. Lewis, and the entire team at Scholastic have been extraordinary and super friendly and just plain cool. Thank you all!

# ABOUT THE AUTHOR

DAN POBLOCKI is the author of several books for young readers, including *The Book of Bad Things*, *The Nightmarys*, *The Stone Child*, and the Mysterious Four series. His recent novels, *The Ghost of Graylock* and *The Haunting of Gabriel Ashe*, were both Junior Library Guild selections and made the American Library Association's Best Fiction for Young Adults list in 2013 and 2014. Dan lives in Brooklyn, where he enjoys the occasional thunderstorm from the comfort of his apartment. Visit him at www.danpoblocki.com.

❖